ALPHA ACADEMY

IF AT FIRST YOU DON'T SUCCEED, YOU'RE NOT AN ALPHA

NAME: *Allie A. Abbott*

AGE: *14 1/2*

HOMETOWN: *Santa Ana, CA*

ACTIVITIES: *Mall model, gifted shopper, rom-com aficionado*

INTERESTS: *Leaving my past behind me.*

TALENT: *Does being genetically gifted count?*

ALPHA AMBITION: *To be more than just a pretty face.*

A
BELLE OF
THE BRAWL

BELLE OF THE BRAWL

AN ALPHAS NOVEL BY LISI HARRISON

poppy

LITTLE, BROWN AND COMPANY
New York   Boston

For Sara Shandler—editor, friend, shrink, alpha.

"OHHMMMMM."

As she sat in full lotus position on a silver blue yoga mat, Charlie Deery's Chap Sticked lips formed a perfect circle as she chanted the sacred sound of the universe. But while her mouth was saying *om*, her mind was screaming *ommmhmuh-gud*. *Scared* had become the new sacred.

She opened one coffee-brown eye and peeked at Alpha Academy's holographic meditation yogi.

"No . . . ohhhhmmmm . . . Peeking . . . ohmmmm," chanted Tran, his lids still blissfully shut. "Keeeep breathing . . . ohmmmmm."

The chubby monk—or "Chunk"—wore a flowing saffron robe and floated a few inches above the Zen Center's meditation pool. Conceived by Shira Brazille, head Alpha and creator of the academy's @-shaped island, Tran's purpose was to teach the girls at the fiercely competitive high school how to relax. And it was completely stressing Charlie out.

The meditation courtyard in the belly of the Buddha-shaped Zen Center should have been a calming respite, but after last night, Charlie wouldn't have been able to find peace at a Woodstock reunion. After one more deep inhalation of jasmine-scented air Charlie gave up.

"Sorry, Tran," she sighed, her mahogany bangs blowing up off her forehead. "I just can't focus."

Tran's puffy cheeks expanded with his smile, slicing his double chin into a quad. His eyes crinkled into crescents as his hologram face flickered out for a split-second and then reappeared. "Buddha says: The way is not in the sky. The way is in the heart."

"I don't even know which way is *up*," Charlie answered, her voice shaken by confusion and stirred with exhaustion. She had spent the night playing ref to an endless wrestling match between her heart and her brain, and still, there was no clear winner in sight.

She lifted her eyes to the patch of blue sky above the meditation courtyard. But instead of neon-colored parrots and personal airplanes, she saw a cloud-shaped Darwin and Allie, each silently imploring her to choose a side—their side.

"You are still looking outside yourself for answers," he said, patting his virtual heart. "Look in."

"*How?*" Charlie asked, her sage-rage mounting.

Tran flickered again. He opened his mouth to speak, but she didn't want to hear it. The only thing Charlie wanted to "look in" was a pint of Tell Me What to Do Before I Go Nuts ice cream. Was he ever going to give her some *real* advice? If not she'd be better off with a Magic 8 Ball. At least that gave answers.

"Namaste," she said, aiming her aPod at his muffin top, and pushing END SESSION. "Namaste," he bowed and then disintegrated.

Now what?

She never should have let Shira connive her into breaking up with Darwin. She never should have convinced Allie to date him so she could keep tabs on him. She never should have confessed to Darwin that the dump was committed under duress. And she never should have stood there when he said he wanted her back. Because she had already promised him to Allie. But was he hers to promise?

Loyalty vs. Love? Head vs. Heart? BFFs vs. BFs? The answer was harder to come by than an iPad 4G.

Charlie unwound her legs from lotus position and reached toward the stone bench where she'd set down her breakfast, a frosted beaker full of a brain-stimulating protein shake specially concocted for invention majors. She placed the silver straw between her lips and took an aggressive sip. Hopefully the ice-cold green goo would cause brain freeze and grant her a moment of much-needed peace. But instead, all the green tea, ginger, and honey blend left behind was the metallic tinge of panic on her tongue and a mild stomachache. *Double now what?*

Charlie pulled out her aPod again and began pacing the perimeter of the meditation courtyard like a caged circus lion. She had one option left. Thumbing the screen she located the Alpha Class Selector app and started to scroll through her options to see what else she could add to her schedule. Overwhelmed by the 322 current courses, Charlie decided to start with the A's and quickly selected Acrobatics, Animation, Arabic, and Astronomy, bringing her total class periods up to eleven. Now she wouldn't have a spare second to fret about her life.

Time	Class	Location
7:30 a.m.	BREAKFAST AND MOTIVATIONAL LECTURE	Pavilion
8:00 a.m.	(RE)INVENTION (IM's ONLY) Mentored lab hour for Alpha experimentation, innovation, motivation.	Marie Curie Invention Laboratory
9:00 a.m.	3-D RENDERING & ANIMATION Create, then replicate. Programs to reproduce your inventions on a global scale.	Melinda Gates Computer Lab
9:40 a.m.	INTRO TO ARABIC Prerequisite: Fluency in Spanish, French, and German	Sculpture Garden
10:10 a.m.	PROTEIN BREAK Nourish your mind and body with a personalized smoothie. Drink fast. Your next class starts in ten minutes.	Health Food Court

10:20 a.m.	THE ART OF EXCELLENCE Betas work to live. Alphas live to work. Map your professional goals with a life coach and plot your path to the top.	Elizabeth I Lecture Hall
11:30 a.m.	HONE IT: FOR WRITERS Whether fact or fiction, when Alphas write, the world reads.	The Fuselage
12:40 p.m.	LUNCH AND SYMPHONY Digest lunch and life as you commune with Beethoven, Brahms, and Tchaikovsky.	Pavilion
1:50 p.m.	GREENER PASTURES Learn how to keep your carbon footprint small while still wearing fabulous shoes.	Vertical Farm
2:55 p.m.	PHYSICS & QUANTUM LEAPS An Alpha in motion stays in motion. Advanced mechanical/philosophical investigations in matter and mind.	Newton's Apple Orchard
4:10 p.m.	ALPHAS THROUGH HISTORY Great women have always risen to the top. Follow their example!	Golda Meir Globe
5:10 p.m.	FIGURE DRAWING It's all in the details. Train your eye and your hands. The spirit will follow.	Sculpture Garden
6:00 p.m.	AERODYNAMIC TRAPEZE Soar to the top of your potential— Alphas dare to fly.	Achilles Track
8:00 p.m.	ASTRONOMY/ASTROLOGY Harness the constellations and reach for the stars.	Delphi Observatory

Setting her aPod down next to what remained of her breakfast, Charlie took a few cautious steps toward the reflection pool and leaned over until she could see herself in the placid water. She shivered and wrapped her arms around her bare shoulders, going over the situation for the hundredth time. Her relationships were tied in more knots than a cable-knit sweater. Wherever she pulled, she would end up with the same result: her life unraveling.

Best friend or boyfriend? Who should she choose? Who would she lose? She turned away from the pool and walked to the Zen garden, a rectangular patch of sand encrusted with polished pink quartz and black obsidian rocks. Picking up a small rake, she began to scratch a list of pros and cons into the sand.

STAY TRUE	ALLIE WHO?
I have a best friend for the first time in my life—and I don't want to lose her.	Darwin is my soul mate. How can I pick a girl I just met over the boy I've loved my entire life?
Enrolling in Alpha Academy is all about making the most of myself. I need to impress Shira, not worry about Darwin!	But how can I be my best self without Darwin, the one person who makes me feel most confident and secure?
If Darwin and I are meant to be it will happen for us . . . someday. Why not let Allie be happy in the short term?	Wait! Darwin doesn't even like Allie. He likes me! Turning him down for Allie won't make a difference for their relationship.
Darwin and I are young. A break might be healthy.	Brakes are only good for one thing—screeching to a stop.

Charlie nibbled her cuticles and studied her list. One wrong yank and the fabric of her life would collapse.

"Buddha? What should I do?" Charlie shouted up through the cavity of the giant deity. Her low, sensible voice struck her as screechy and desperate as it echoed off the hammered-silver walls. "I need a sign. And I need it fast." She turned in a slow circle, like a satellite searching for a signal. A bird passed over the open sky above—was that the sign? Was it telling her to leave? Charlie bit her lip and struggled to interpret it, but it was so vague.

Ping!

A text from Buddha! How very modern.

She ran to her aPod.

Allie: Where R U? Hash browns at brkfst!

A slow smile spread across her face.

"Thanks, Buddha," Charlie whispered, stepping out into the tropical sunshine of Alpha Island. She yanked the elastic out of her ponytail and liberated her brown waves. She had her answer. She finally knew what to do. The only question left was: could she go through with it?

2

APOD MESSAGE
TO ALL STUDENTS AND FACULTY
SUNDAY, SEPTEMBER 26TH
5:00 P.M.

FEEL THE BREEZE?

CHANGE IS IN THE AIR.

ASSEMBLY AT THE PAVILION.

6:00 P.M.

DON'T BE LATE!

—SHIRA

3

Hurrying down the gravel path between the dorms and the Pavilion, brushing past palm fronds, giant ferns, and fragrant plumeria, Allie A. Abbott's heart was soaring like the wings of the phoenix-shaped building in front of her. Surrounded by Alphas in their school uniforms—clear gladiator sandals, balloon-sleeved button-down shirts, and pleated metallic miniskirts that twinkled in the twilight— Allie may not have been among friends, exactly, but at least she wasn't in disguise anymore. Her blond hair was back, navy blue eyes no longer hid behind fake green contact lenses, and she'd finally rebooted her golden tan. A beauty must-have she was forced to sacrifice while pretending to be Allie J. Abbott the pasty eco-maniac who accused her of stealing sun from the flowers . . . along with her identity. Unfortunately, the identity part was true. But oh, well. That was more behind her than the butt floss she proudly called underwear. The days of wearing recycled granny panties were over.

Over the past couple of months, Allie's self-esteem had congealed faster than food court Chinese food. The image of her boyfriend Fletcher and best friend Trina making out had been burned into the pleasure center of her brain. But now the burn was starting to scab over and Allie could put her energy toward scar-free healing. No more crying over the pieces of her broken heart. No more posing as Allie J. Abbott, the mega-famous folksinger whose acceptance letter she had accidentally received in the mail. No more black hair and bare feet. She had Charlie now. She had Darwin. She had hope.

"Move it, *beta*," breathed Olivia Dufrenidis in Allie's ear as she barreled past her toward the doors of the Pavilion. Olivia was a tall, D-cup, Greek olive-oil heiress who at age fourteen founded the Dufrenidis Report, a blog that broke more political news stories than Perez Hilton broke celebrity gossip. Ever since Allie's lie had been revealed, Olivia went out of her way to bully her. Allie's breath hitched in her throat for a second as she absorbed the insult. *Beta* was the worst thing you could call someone at Alpha Academy.

"Sorry," Allie muttered, clenching her teeth as Olivia's departing platform wedges kicked gravel onto her legs. But like the pebbles hitting her ankles, Allie reminded herself, names only hurt for a split-second. *Keep it together, Al.*

There were a lot of reasons Allie should have been a basket case. In August, she'd caught her boyfriend Fletcher cheating on her with her best friend, Trina. But that was only the beginning. Next, she'd committed identity fraud by faking her way into Shira's school for overachievers. A few weeks later, Allie's true identity was discovered and the real Allie J enrolled in the Academy. Now most girls at Alpha Academy thought she was a liar, a joke, or worse. But Allie had *survived*. That was what mattered. Shira had let her stay at Alpha Academy to try to prove herself, to find her passion and roll with it. And her housemates Charlie and Skye had recently forgiven her lies and impersonation. Thank God, because Allie needed to know she could count on Charlie and Skye to be there for her—especially now that the rest of the school wasn't.

She squinted up through the blazing orange sunset at the Pavilion, its brise-soleil shades retracting on either side of the tall oblong structure like enormous white steel wings. Then she pulled out the small bottle of Purell she always carried and squirted it onto her hands, feeling instantly calmer when the germ-killing smell hit her nostrils.

Where were Charlie and Skye? Allie craned her neck, looking around for her friends like a puppy searching for its littermates. They'd both been in overdrive all weekend, trying to impress Shira by working extra-hard in their classes and even adding more courses to their schedules. Allie should be following their lead, but finding your passion wasn't like shopping for a party dress or a new bag—endless browsing wouldn't necessarily get her any closer to unlocking her potential or uncovering a talent. And here at Alpha Academy, there weren't any salespeople at the ready to help her with her search. Girls like Skye and Charlie had talent. All Allie had was a class schedule packed tighter than Ugly Betty in a pair of Spanx, and still she was no closer to self-discovery. She knew she had something more to offer than personal style and stellar taste . . . didn't she?

Allie's sun-kissed shoulders were jostled by the other Alphas crowding through the rounded glass doors and into the shiny white room. The space buzzed with excitement as Alphas began to look up. Above their heads were 3–D holograms of fish, whales, and giant cruise ships. A shimmering banner cascaded from one white wall to another, zooming up to the ceiling, then passing through the crowd of Alphas in a glittery rush.

YOU ARE INVITED TO SET SAIL ON THE ALPHA MUSE CRUISE
SWIM IN THE SEA OF INSPIRATION WITH THE ALPHA MUSES
OCTOBER EIGHTH, 7 P.M., THE ALPHA CRUISE SHIP

A shiver of excitement rippled along Allie's spine. It would be amazing to get off Shira's tiny woman-made island, even if it was only for a two-hour boat ride. The place was a paradise in many ways, but Allie often felt as if she were trapped in a crowded elevator stuck between floors. Allie scanned the bleachers for Skye or Charlie, but before she found them, the unmistakable sound of a guitar stopped her in her tracks.

"I'm going to play a little song for y'all," said a scratchy voice, belonging to Allie's housemate Allie J—or AJ, as she liked to be called.

AJ stood on one of the ergonomic white egg chairs, dominating the crowd in spite of her tiny 5'2" stature. Her scraggly black hair was tucked into a crocheted green tam that sat sagging on her head like a giant mushroom. With her vampire-pale skin and emaciated frame, she reminded Allie of the annoying hippie chick who worked at Bulgur 'N Beetz, a health-food sandwich shop back in Santa Ana. Why did health food freaks always look so sickly? Wasn't it kind of an oxymoron?

AJ stood holding her guitar like a machine gun aimed straight at Allie. She narrowed her moss-green eyes, flashing a micro-smile that sent Allie's stomach to her gladiators.

"Sing it, sister!" shouted Tameeka Sands, a slam poet with her own line of designer skateboards.

"Go, AJ! Break it down!" echoed Gweneviere Stulz, an urban farmer and the founder of a group of radical agriculture reformers called the Ronald McDon'ts.

"My newest song is called 'Identity Theft,'" AJ drawled.

"It's inspired by a situation close to my heart. Too close!" The crowd giggled, and a few girls looked at Allie before turning back to AJ.

Serious-leh? Can't we move on? Allie wanted to scream. When would AJ finally let this drop? AJ's war on Allie had already dragged on longer than the battle sequence in *Avatar*.

Allie spun on one heel and tried to get as far away as possible, but she couldn't move fast enough to block out AJ's lame lyrics.

Identity theft. Identity theft.
I offer you a piece of me
Every time I write a song,
Allie abused my generosity
And girlfriend, that's just wrong!

When you sing the things that come from my soul,
I do not feel bereft,
But take my name, my eyes, my mole—
Well, that's identity theft!

A salty knot of emotion welled up in Allie's throat. She squeezed her eyes shut and shook her head slightly in a desperate attempt to quell the hot tears that threatened to escape her eye sockets and fall down her cheeks, wishing she could close her ears just as tightly. Being hated was one thing, but having everyone *sing* about it was unbearable.

> *Identity theft. Identity theft.*
> *An imposter and a faker.*
> *Nothing real, nothing true*
> *Like a plagiarized English paper!*

> *Identity theft. Identity theft.*
> *Stop, thief! Empty your sack!*
> *Keep my wallet, keep my purse.*
> *It's the personality I want back!*

Allie's moist eyes landed on Thalia, her house muse, seated in an empty cluster of ergonomic egg-shaped chairs to her left. AJ and her chorus line took seats across the round room, but Allie plopped down next to Thalia instead.

The muse's golden irises shone with amusement, and her honey-blond hair caught the last rays of the orange sun as it sank behind the shades. "A change of scenery should be nice, don't you think?"

"That's an understatement," Allie muttered, making accidental eye contact with AJ, who glowered at her across the room.

"Allie, a wise woman once said: Nobody can go back and start a new beginning, but anyone can start today and make a new ending." Thalia put her huge former basketball player's paw over Allie's and squeezed.

Before Allie could protest, a round glass door slid open from the back of the room. Darwin walked through it, his sandy hair falling over his left eye. Even though he'd dumped her after her impersonation went public, somehow, the less she saw of him, the more irresistible he got. Today, he was wearing a white sweatshirt, navy board shorts, and flip-flops, and his light brown hair was damp. Had he come from the beach?

She pasted on a smile that she hoped looked non-desperate, non-needy, cute yet mysterious, and waited for his eyes to find her. Darwin whispered something in Taz's ear and the three boys took seats in the last row. Allie shook out her waves and counted down in her head, willing him to spot her.

Five, four, three, two, one!

Darwin's eyes—hazel with flecks of gold and green—made contact with her navy blue ones and sent an electric spark traveling from Allie's scalp to her toes. Allie returned his gaze and smiled. She wiggled her fingers at him in a quick, almost imperceptible wave. Darwin smiled back and chin-thrusted a quick hello, before his eyes boomeranged away from her and back to his brother.

Allie sat back in her egg chair and felt a secret smile playing on her lips. AJ might have been a big fish in a small pond, but Allie was about to snag the biggest catch of all.

THE PAVILION
HALF MOON THEATER
SUNDAY, SEPTEMBER 26TH
5:59 P.M.

Late as usual and breathing hard, Skye Hamilton burst headlong through the assembly doors. She spun her slender body around in a graceful pirouette and quickly assessed the crowded room, scanning the semicircle of shiny white bleachers in search of the Jackie O's. Her gaze automatically rose higher until she caught herself and lowered her head, remembering to avoid looking at the top row where the Brazille brothers always sat.

Alphas clustered with their housemates, each group nervously buzzing about tonight's mysterious assembly and the billboards for the Muse Cruise—whatever that was. The Oprahs sat in a huddle toward the back, the Mother Teresas favored front row center. She waved a quick hello to her fellow dancers, Tweety and Ophelia, ensconced in the J. K. Rowling section. Then Skye's searching gaze landed squarely on AJ (what was that hideous thing on her head?)

18

sitting cross-legged on her egg chair to the left of the stage, flanked by the Beyoncés on one side and the Hillary Clintons on the other. She flashed her housemate a tight smile and moved closer.

"Where are the rest of the Jackie O's?" Skye asked, still trying to catch her breath.

AJ pointed an unmanicured finger toward the other side of the round stage. Charlie and Allie both wave-pointed at a seat they'd saved for her. Skye smiled, wiping a cool trickle of dance-sweat from her temple.

"Thanks," Skye muttered to AJ. She sashayed across the round stage to join her friends, flipping her white-blond wavelets over her shoulder. "See ya."

"There's no law that we have to sit with our houses," AJ called after her, but Skye rolled her eyes and kept walking, pretending not to hear. Instead, she waved to Allie, who looked a little teary sitting next to Charlie and Thalia. Poor Allie. Why couldn't AJ just let the drama die already? Skye flashed Allie a reassuring smile, then plopped into the seat next to Charlie, folding her leg warmer–clad calves to one side of her seat and leaning in to whisper to her housemates.

"Sooo . . . What'd I miss? Why are we here?" She sent a stealth sideways glance at the back row for a brief Brazille-brothers assessment before returning to her fellow O's. But she wasn't sneaky enough, because Sydney—

Shira's most sensitive son—flashed her a desperate smile. Skye turned away and picked a tuft of imaginary lint from her champagne-colored dance skirt.

"Good question." Charlie shrugged, her mocha-brown eyes twinkling under her bangs. "Shira hasn't yelled at us in seventy-two hours?"

For the last seventy-two hours, Skye had been in dance overdrive, logging twelve-hour solo dance days with only the holographic playback machine to keep her company. Ever since Shira had called her into her office last week for a little pep talk wrapped around a death threat, Skye had been a dancing machine. Partly, she wanted to improve her moves and impress the bossy Aussie, but mainly, Skye had made a deal with the she-devil: If Skye broke Syd's heart, Shira would break Skye's enrollment at Alpha Academy.

But Syd's heart was made of fine china that cracked and fissured with every beat. He was walking PMS, and to make matters worse, Skye's heart insisted on beating loudly for a different Brazille brother—Taz. Skye had tried to force her heart to follow orders, but loving Syd was something she just couldn't do.

And those who can't do, hide.

As Skye curled up in her chair and tried to ignore Syd's eyes drilling hearts into her back, a silence fell over the room. The circular stage slid open silently to reveal Shira Brazille. The mogul's head slowly rose up from the stage, starting with her kinky auburn curls piled high atop her crown and followed by her ubiquitous round sunglasses that hid her ice-blue eyes from view. Next came her yoga-toned shoulders—one bare, one covered with brightly patterned fabric, then finally the rest of her, clad in a flowing Pucci patio dress. Balancing atop a BRAZILLE INDUSTRIES–emblazoned white hoverdisc, Shira floated in midair a few inches above the closing hatch of the stage.

"Hello, m'dears," Shira boomed, her red lips widening into a TV-ready smile.

"For once, none of us is in danger," Charlie whispered, leaning in so Allie and Skye could hear.

Depends what you mean by danger. Skye did a few calming neck-rolls and waited for Shira to go on.

"First off, I'd like Singh Rootlieb and Saylene Davenport to take the stage." The room erupted in whispers as two girls stood up. Both of them wore sunglasses. Alphas in each row took out their aPods and aimed them at the petite Indian from the Virginia Woolf house and the broad-shouldered Texan from the Tyra house. Dozens of muffled bleeps meant girls were downloading personal data using the aPod Alpha Bios app.

"They're both IM's!" Charlie whispered as Singh and Saylene took the stage.

"What's with the shades?" Allie whispered. Charlie shrugged.

21

Skye turned to look at Thalia. The muse avoided eye contact and stared straight ahead. *She knows something.*

"These two Alphas, both invention majors"—Shira swept her bling-encrusted hand toward both girls before continuing—"took a very big risk. They teamed up to create SeeVD's—sunglasses that play movies. The lenses act as mini-LCD screens, and if used correctly might bring humans one step closer to perfect fusion with technology. I love risk-takers. That's why you're all here—to take risks! Risks move society forward. They advance our species."

Get to the point, Shira.

Singh and Saylene's smiles were wide enough to park a yacht as they stood onstage, awkwardly receiving Shira's gushing praise.

"But." Shira's expression hardened. Her smile flattened into a thin line. "They made a careless error. The lenses were not properly coated, and they singed the girls' eyelashes off."

Ah-ha! Skye snuck a look at Allie and they both struggled to suppress nervous giggles at the horrible explanation for the girls' shades.

Shira cleared her throat. "And then, what did they do? Did these two promising Alphas start afresh, with a renewed enthusiasm?"

Skye stared at her cuticles.

"NO." Shira hate-stared at Singh and Saylene like they

were cockroaches and she was about to unleash a bug bomb. The smiles disappeared from their faces. "They *cried.* Just like they are doing now." Shira waved her arms wildly, reminding Skye of the monkey bats in *The Wizard of Oz.* The two girls onstage started shaking and began to wipe away silent tears streaming down their cheeks.

"So . . . that's all?" Skye leaned over and whispered to Charlie, raising her white eyebrows.

Charlie gave Skye a knowing look. "Shira hates crying. She thinks it's weak."

The mogul went on. "Crying is a waste of good mascara. Failure should make you *try*, not *cry*. And therefore, Singh and Saylene, I am afraid I must ask you to pack your bags and board your Personal Alpha Planes. You are both going home."

"But Shira!" The Texan took off her sunglasses and revealed red, puffy eyelids the size of kneecaps. *Ew!* The room inhaled in a collective gasp.

"No buts. You no longer qualify as Alphas. Therefore, you no longer belong here."

As the crowed erupted in shocked whispers and girls began adding two more names to the growing list in their aPods of girls who'd been kicked out of the Academy, the two half-blind IM's shame-shuffled out of the room.

Shira continued once the commotion died down: "The only person I've ever heard cry for a good reason is my special, sensitive, *poetic* son Sydney. And thanks to a very special Alpha in the making, that's become a thing of the past, too."

Ohmuhgud. Skye's heart began to beat faster than a Cascada song. She pulled her metallic silver hoodie up over her hair, wishing she could disappear. But a cotton-Lycra hood was no match for a Shira-induced spotlight.

"And because my son is happy for the first time in his life, I have decided to let him continue associating with this very special girl."

Oh please no. Skye squeezed her turquoise eyes shut, her ears tingling with mortification-anticipation. When the entire assembly discovered she was Syd's girlfriend, her reputation would be ground into dust. She would be known as Puffs the Magic Tissue for the rest of the year!

But shutting her eyes couldn't stop the impending shout-out any more than Dorothy could stop the tornado from ripping her out of Kansas. "Skye Hamilton, please stand."

A hot shame-blush crept up her neck. Skye clung pathetically to her egg chair as if it could keep her from drowning in the floodwaters of embarrassment. Slowly, she pulled her hood down and rose out of her seat, pasting a fake smile on her bright red face.

Skye normally loved an opportunity to have all eyes on her, but not this time. She turned toward the back of the room, where Syd stood, applauding, his skinny jeans and frayed gray T-shirt, messy brown-black hair, and brooding good looks not obscuring the fact that he was beaming at her like a new bride.

Skye waved feebly at him, cringing inwardly as he pursed his lips into an air-kiss. She looked at Taz, whose bright blue eyes were as vacant as a haunted motel. He looked up and caught Skye's gaze for a second, raising one eyebrow as his mouth twisted into a mocking smirk. But before Skye could communicate anything in return, he looked back down at his phone.

It's not what you think! Skye wanted to shout. She wished she could explain, but she was trapped between a jock and a soft place.

"Skye Hamilton is a great example of how to have a relationship with a boy without sacrificing your ambitions. Instead of rubbing noses with my son all weekend, she was hard at work in the dance studio, keeping her toes—and her priorities—in line."

Can I sit now?

"And because of Skye, I am lifting the ban."

Huh?

Every row in the auditorium rippled like sea grass as the eighty-odd remaining Alphas tried to figure out what Shira's announcement meant. The ban on parental phone calls? The ban on pop culture from the world beyond Alpha Island? The ban on non-reflective clothing? Skye seized the confusion as an opportunity to sit, curling into her egg chair and waiting for Shira to clarify.

"From this moment forward, consider the ban on the Brazille Boys lifted. You may"—Shira wrung her hands, searching for the right word. "You may *socialize* with my sons outside of class."

Ohmuhgud!

The cylindrical room erupted with scream-claps. Everywhere Skye looked, she saw smiling Alphas shrieking, giggling, and bouncing out of their seats with excitement. Skye looked at Charlie and Allie, but both of them sat silently.

"But!" Shira boomed, quieting the hysterical crowd in the bleachers. "Anyone who puts the pursuit of a boy before her studies will be sent home. A true Alpha knows that boys are toys—only to be played with after the important things are done. G'night, lollies. And remember, I'll be watching you. If you stick to your studies, you'll all enjoy the privilege of attending an inspirational evening organized by your muses on the Brazille Industries cruise ship. October eighth—mark your calendars!"

At that, the panel on the stage slid open again and Shira descended into the island's rabbit warren–like network of interconnected underground tunnels.

Skye shot her aquamarine eyes over the hysterical heads of her fellow Alphas and searched the back row. Syd was already headed her way. Dingo ran toward the door, looking terrified as a gaggle of giggling girls chanted his name and ran after him.

"What's up, ladies?" Taz opened his gym-perfect arms wide and showed more teeth than a great white shark. In seconds, a swarm of girls surrounded him.

Ugh!

It was times like this when Skye wished she could ask her mother, famous Russian ballerina Natasha Flailenkoff, for advice. But Shira forbade all phone calls to the outside. The one piece of her mother Skye carried with her to the Academy was her HAD (hopes and dreams) slipper, a purple satin toe shoe that Natasha said would bring her luck. So far, Skye had written down ten HADs on tiny scraps of paper and kept them stashed inside the toe shoe's secret compartment.

Skye sighed as Syd made his way toward her through the excited crowd of girls. Unlike his brother, he was a one-woman kind of guy. And soon, she sighed inwardly, he would be hanging by her side like a limp sleeve.

HAD No. 11: Find a way to be sleeveless by next weekend.

5

Standing next to Charlie, whose Sultan Sea Mud Mask had dried to make her face look like ancient pottery, Allie stared glumly at her pores in the bathroom mirror. Now that she'd ditched her skunky black hair and skanky green contacts, the beauty she'd always taken for granted stared back at her. But if she looked so good, why was Darwin avoiding her?

Chewing her lower lip, Allie stuck her head into the face-shaped indentation on the vanity mirror and waited for it to take a bio-scan of her pores. Seconds later, a British voice said, "Now dispensing vitamin C scrub with algae crystals. Apply in circular strokes over T-zone."

Allie put her hands beneath a small A-shaped plastic spout and caught a big poof of cleanser. It looked like blue Cool Whip. As she massaged it in little circles over her face, Skye and Triple Threat (her threats being dancer, model,

28

and actress, her real name being Andrea, and her presence being reliably annoying) walked in.

Triple was going on about Skye's party-girl ways finally paying off, but Skye didn't seem to agree.

"Tell her, Claymation," Triple lunged into a deep hamstring stretch and thrust her strong jaw toward Charlie, winking one golden, almond-shaped eye.

"*Tellerwhat?*" Charlie asked, the mask causing her to slur each word together.

"How she's like the Neil Armstrong of this school! One giant step for womankind." Triple smirk-smiled at Skye. "Not that I'm walking on the moon, mind you. Boys are a bad idea for those of us who are truly destined for greatness."

"So . . . you and Syd, huh?" asked Allie, rinsing the algae scrub off her cheeks, ignoring Triple's outsized ego.

Skye's turquoise eyes met Allie's in the mirror. She looked scared and tired. "Um, yeah. Me and Syd. It's not that serious. We might break up."

"I can't believe Shira's dropping the ban. I never saw this coming," said Charlie, wiping her mask off with a wet washcloth and sending muddy flakes flying onto the bathroom's silver foam floors.

A catty smile spread over Triple's perfectly proportioned face as she pushed a purple button in the wall designed to turn the bathroom into a steam bath. Soon, eucalyptus-scented steam shot out from ten tiny vents in the walls. "Did you guys hear what Ophelia did to try to lure Dingo? She reprogrammed one of the billboards in the Pavilion to say DINGOPHELIA: THE NEW BRANGELINA and beamed it into the sky over the Brazille house."

"Oh no!" Skye scream-gasped, covering her mouth as if she'd witnessed a flirting crime of epic proportions. "It sounds like a disease."

"She's obvious-leh desperate," Allie commented.

Just then AJ walked through the open door into the steamy bathroom, pulling her crocheted green tam from her head and letting her scraggly black hair fall down her back. "Everyone knows *subtlety* is key when bagging a bro," AJ added.

"You don't exactly radiate subtlety, AJ." Allie spat back.

The folksinger narrowed her murky green eyes and made a face like she'd just tasted something sour. "Um, Skye? What rhymes with pathetic?"

Skye shot her toothbrush into the air like a baton. "Balletic!" She executed a quick twirl to illustrate the word.

"Thanks, Skye," Allie giggled. "AJ can't stop writing songs about me. Hey AJ," Allie went on, gaining courage, "why do you keep wearing that hat everywhere? Isn't it illegal?"

"I got permission from Shira," AJ snapped. "It's my creative cap. I use it when I'm in writing mode."

"It's not Shira I'm worried about. It's the fashion police. You're wanted for fugliness all over the island."

Skye and Triple snort-giggled through mouthfuls of toothpaste.

AJ turned on her heel and headed back to the bedroom. The others followed a few minutes later, leaving Allie alone to stare at the mirror. Even without any makeup on, she knew she was prettier than 99 percent of the population. Her heart-shaped face, button nose, and wide mouth had gotten her modeling work in catalogues for years. But at Alpha Academy, most girls were beautiful. And Alpha girls had what Allie lacked: a talent that they'd been pursuing for their whole lives. Something they were the best at.

Allie sighed, breathing in the eucalyptus-scented air. Then she grabbed her aPod, resting next to the sink on the bathroom counter, and stabbed the GPS icon with an eager finger. She typed D-A-R-W-I-N into the navigation bar and waited for her aPod to find him so she could, too.

Ping!

Seriousleh? Allie's eyebrows jumped in surprise. The blue GPS locator dot showed Darwin was only fifty feet away, in the rose garden just south of Jackie O.

Allie's heart did a cartwheel. Darwin had come to see her!

She whirled around to face the mirror again for a quick once-over. Teeth: spinach-free. Hair: wavy-cute. Lips:

slightly chapped. She smeared a coat of tinted lip gloss across her rosebud mouth, adjusted her shiny platinum pj's, pinched her cheeks, and barreled through the Jackie O bedroom and down the spiral glass staircase.

At the last second, she grabbed a blue glass vase stuffed with four bird-of-paradise flowers. Clutching the vase, she slipped on a pair of flip-flops and slid quietly out the door.

The hybrid garden was sandwiched between the Jackie O and Queen Elizabeth houses, and was encircled by an ivy-covered brick wall. Allie pushed the gate open and looked around, sniffing the air in the hope of catching a whiff of cinnamon. Her heart was beating like the wings of the hummingbirds that flitted among the exotic flowers. "Anyone here?"

"Oh, it's *you.*"

Allie turned toward the voice and nearly ran into Darwin. His light-brown hair shone in the moonlight, and his soulful hazel eyes blinked rapidly in surprise. *How cute—he's nervous!* The thought put Allie at ease, and she straightened her posture, holding the blue vase in front of her with both hands.

She smiled her best easy-breezy catalogue grin. "Hi."

"Hi." Darwin held a fistful of hot pink peonies, each bloom the size of a soccer ball. His cheeks were almost as pink as the flowers.

"Are those for me?" Allie reached out and took the

flowers, noticing they smelled like cotton candy. Allie delicately plucked a petal off its stem and put it in her mouth, grinning as it dissolved on her tongue like pink cotton candy.

Darwin remained silent. *Where was his un-mute button?*

"I'm really glad you came. It's so great we can be out in the open now," she babbled, dumping the bird-of-paradise flowers onto the ground. "Your mom has perfect timing, don't you think? Now we can start over. We don't have to hide!" She stuck the peonies in the blue vase with a flourish, as if now that she had the flowers it was official: She and Darwin were *back*.

"Allie," Darwin sighed, staring down at the phosphorescent moss covering the ground, glowing patches of neon green and yellow. He shook his head slightly. "We need to talk."

Allie cut him off, her heart soaring, wanting to skip over any awkward, tortured conversations about their breakup. That was old news. "Yeah, I know we do. I am so sorry about what I did. Pretending to be AJ, lying, everything. But I'm so happy you've decided to forgive me. Now we can really get to know—"

"Allie—"

"Sorry. Go ahead." Allie smiled, hoping this awkward phase of their relationship wouldn't last long. She was already imagining taking pictures with Shira's cutest progeny, and somehow breaking through the firewall so they'd end up in her ex-boyfriend Fletcher's inbox.

Darwin's eyes made contact with hers, but instead of mirroring her excitement, they projected uncertainty. What was going on?

"Listen," he said. "We're not going to start fresh. Things between us are over."

Over? Allie's blue eyes filled with tears. Her heart ached beneath her metallic clothing. She looked down uncomprehendingly at the flowers. "What?"

"I'm sorry." Darwin's voice was firm. Allie's overworked brain tried to process what was going on. Why the flowers? Why was he here?

"You came all the way here . . . for nothing?" She waved the vase around and one of the flowers tipped out, falling to the ground. A ball of pain began to form in her stomach, like that time the Jamba Juice at her mall got a shipment of bad berries. And suddenly she realized. "Ohmuhgud, *of course*," she hissed. "I guess now that your mom's loosened up the rules, you plan on pulling a *Bachelor* and giving a flower to every girl in school!"

"That's not it. You don't underst—"

"I understand plenty," Allie cut him off. Suddenly her head was swimming, and the sweet smell of cotton candy flowers made her nauseous. Her dinner was rising in her stomach.

Before Darwin could say another word, Allie shoved the vase into his chest and let go, turning to push her way out of the crowded garden. Through a veil of tears, the colors of all the plants looked like a circus, and she was the star sideshow attraction. *Allie Abbott! Come one, come all, and watch as her heart breaks into a million pieces!*

6

Wrapped tighter than a Thai spring roll in her pearl-white comforter, Charlie watched the minutes tick by on the illuminated digits of her aPod. She slept in the exact center of the room's horseshoe arrangement of beds. To her right lay Triple Threat, snoring lightly, and to her left were Allie and Skye, both passed out on their stomachs, their backs rising slightly with each inhalation. On the other side of Triple, AJ lay in her bed surrounded by pens and notebooks, curled into a tiny ball on her side. Charlie clutched her aPod tightly in her hand, letting out a silent sigh when the digits turned to 11:29 p.m. Every year, for as long as Charlie could remember, she'd celebrated this moment. Because September 26 at 11:29 p.m. was when Darwin was born.

In the past, they'd celebrated it together, making a wish, just as they did on Charlie's birthday. But now everything

36

involving Darwin contained seeds of trouble, about to sprout up and devour Charlie like a carnivorous plant.

Even so, just because Charlie wasn't with Darwin now didn't mean she couldn't make a wish. She gazed up at the constellations visible through the glass ceiling of the Jackie O bedroom and wondered what she should wish for: that Darwin would stop loving her? That Allie would stop liking him? That Darwin would love her but not show it until Allie had moved on to someone who loved her back? Yeah, that was it!

"Please make Darwin stop loving me until . . ." She whispered, but before she could finish her wish, the numbers changed. Did that mean that Darwin was going to stop loving her?

The thought of Darwin giving up on her simultaneously turned Charlie's stomach and cleared her head. She'd gotten used to being without Darwin, to concentrating on herself and her projects at the lab. After all, if Allie found out Darwin had chosen Charlie over her, she'd suffer from PTSD—Post Trina Stress Disorder. And Charlie would lose her best friend.

Bzzzz!

Another text arrived on Charlie's muted aPod.

Darwin: I'm waiting.

Darwin had been texting Charlie all night, saying he'd wait for her in the hybrid garden's greenhouse for as long as it took. Charlie sat up a tiny bit in her mummy-wrap and looked around the room. Everyone seemed to be sleeping soundly now, so there was no excuse left. She had to go and meet him.

Charlie silently slipped a hoodie over her pj's, grabbed a pair of clear gladiator sandals, and padded cautiously down the spiral staircase. When she reached the door to Jackie O, she gasped for air, her heart doing a soft-shoe shuffle of excitement and trepidation. Her resolution in the belly of the Buddha still held—she couldn't sell out Allie right now, not even for Darwin. But there was no way she could stand in front of him and actually say it. His hazel eyes and gorgeous smile—adorably dimpled on just one cheek—still had the power to melt her into a puddle. How could a puddle tell Darwin no?

"Be strong," she whispered to herself as she walked down the gravel path under a bright midnight moon. "Do it for Allie." Pressing her lips together in a determined line, Charlie pushed open the iron gate of the hybrid garden and headed for the glass structure at its center.

The greenhouse flickered from the outside, and when Charlie walked through the door, she saw something written in red, pink, white, and orange peony petals. She squinted down at it in the dim glow of the candles, reminding herself to be strong and stick to her plan.

D + C
4 EVER

Darwin stepped out of the shadows. "Like it?"

Charlie grinned, her coffee-brown eyes locked with Darwin's hazel ones in an eye-embrace that felt as comfortable as flannel sheets. She curled her toes and kept her feet planted, fighting her instinct to run over to him and wrap her arms around his ropy shoulders. Suddenly, a wave of paranoia washed over her, and she shook her head slightly to try to flick it away. What if Allie had heard her and was lurking in the garden somewhere, spying on them?

Charlie's throat felt like it was stuffed with tube socks. *Now or never.* Resolved to put the brakes on Darwin's speeding car, she rushed over to the rose petal heart and scraped her feet across it, scattering the petals in the dirt.

Darwin looked at her confused.

"I'm sorry, Darwin, but . . ." She paused, looking at the petal-strewn grass. "I can't."

"What? I don't understand. . . ." Darwin's voice was husky, strangled with hurt. "You heard my mom tonight. We don't have to hide anymore." He walked over to Charlie and pushed a sun-bleached thatch of hair out of his face, then moved to grab her hand in his.

But Charlie twisted her hand out of his grasp. "We can't. *I* can't." Charlie couldn't bring herself to look him in the eye after getting the words out, so she stared miserably at the burgundy tips of his Pumas and swallowed hard. "I can't risk hurting Allie."

Darwin reached out and cupped Charlie's chin, forcing her to meet his gaze. His eyes, normally calmer than the Caribbean Sea, were glassy with emotion. "You're telling me you're choosing Allie's feelings over mine? After everything that's happened—"

"I've never had a real friend before, Darwin," she said, as if that explained everything. Because in a way, it did.

Charlie was practically shaking now, just like the flames of the candles, their reflection dancing on the glass walls of the greenhouse. She took a rose-filled breath and went on. "She was so upset tonight, Darwin. You should have seen her."

"Charlie, the girl impersonated a celebrity and lied to the whole school for three weeks! How deep can her feelings be? She'll get over this. Remember when Mel had a crush on that bossa nova singer in Sao Paulo? He still can't listen to jazz, but he discovered country and fell for Taylor Swift. Allie will discover . . . country, too," he finished lamely, probably realizing his analogy made no sense.

Or did it?

Charlie was about to tell him this wasn't the same thing at all . . . that Allie was different . . . that she couldn't just distract her with someone else . . . when she realized: Maybe she *could*.

"That's it." A smile broke across her face like a lightning bolt.

"What?"

"Mel! Allie should hook up with Mel!" Charlie paced around one of the rosebud-covered tables, twirling a mahogany curl around her finger the way she always did when she needed to concentrate. A smile began to spread across her lips. Allie looked a whole lot like Mel's Brazilian crush. Same dark blond waves, same tan, same dramatic blue eyes. And from everything Allie had told her about Fletcher, Mel was *exactly* her type. He was into clothes and shopping, he was objectively adorable by anyone's standards, and he was just unattainable enough to keep Allie's interest. If Allie fell for Mel, she wouldn't care that Charlie and Darwin were an item again. And maybe, just maybe, Mel would prove to be Allie's soul mate the way Darwin was Charlie's. It was a win-win-win-win!

Charlie relayed all this to Darwin, but after he'd heard her out, he rocked back on his heels and shook his head, crossing his arms protectively over his sweatshirt. "You know who you sound like?"

"A super-smart girl who has just solved everyone's problems?" Charlie grinned.

"No. You sound like my mom. Manipulative. Controlling. Scheming." Darwin sighed and shook his head again.

"Your mom's not all bad. She did manage to build this whole island, after all. Not to mention an empire. And you." Charlie blush-grinned and saw that Darwin would let himself be convinced. She just had to push the right buttons. "Just trust me, Darwin. I want us to be together. This is the only way."

Darwin's kissable lips lifted in a genuine smile, and Charlie felt her heart lifting, too.

After all, Darwin was a practical guy. Charlie knew he couldn't resist a good investment. Especially since theirs was a future worth waiting for.

7

Skye settled her tired back against the massage bench of the day spa steam room, her posture relaxing as the steam soothed her aching calves. Like Tweety and Ophelia, who lay on either side of her, each on her own massage table. A heat-activated towel wrapped tightly around her torso sent targeted tea-tree gel deep into her pores. She took a deep breath as the bench's auto-shiatsu targeted her neck, and closed her Tiffany box–blue eyes. Sighing deeply, Skye swept first one taut leg and then the other in a wide circle through the opaque air, wiggling her freshly pedi'd toes.

This should have been the perfect end to her day. She'd had a great dance class: Triple was still their instructor Mimi's favorite dancer, but Mimi hadn't stopped to humiliate or yell at Skye during class this time. It was a glissade in the right direction. But Skye was drowning in

43

other worries, and her ocean of anxiety was so turbulent that even a change of heart from Mimi couldn't calm the waters.

"So now that we're finally alone," trilled Tweety, a petite olive-skinned brunette with a birdlike voice. "We're waiting for the dirt on you and Syd."

Skye sighed, unfastening her platinum wavelets from their coil on the top of her head and letting her hair fall around her shoulders. Now that her hair was free, maybe she'd finally be able to confess her real feelings. "The truth?"

"Don't leave anything out!" Ophelia grunted from the other bench. Skye could see her flame-red bun wiggling through the white of the steam as she executed an endless series of Pilates crunches.

Skye closed her eyes again and tried to organize her crazy thoughts into something coherent. If she told the bun-heads, would it get back to Shira? Could Skye afford to take the risk?

"Syd must be super-intense, like Altoids after a week of Doublemint," purred Tweety, flipping over on her massage table to do a quick cow-cat yoga sequence.

"He's intense, all right," Skye spat bitterly, then continued in a flat voice. "Intensely annoying!"

Both bun-heads sat up in the thick steam, sensing they'd hit more dirt than they'd known to dig for.

Skye wrapped her slender, toned arms around her

own shoulders and gave herself a pity-hug. "I'm totally into Taz. But Shira caught me on camera breaking things off with Syd. The camera showed us together, and Syd was acting happy, so Shira put two and two together and came up with five! She thinks Syd and I are a perfect couple, and she said that if I ever hurt her son, she'd send me home."

Once a chunk of Skye's internal dam was chipped away, the whole river of truth came rushing out. Skye took a deep breath of hot steam after spilling her guts, and noticed that she already felt better. She still had Syd hanging over her like a cement cardigan, but now at least she wasn't hiding it from everyone. Tweety and Ophelia weren't the sharpest knives in the drawer, but maybe they'd be able to help Skye devise a solution, or at least provide an umbrella during the storm.

"So . . . you got back together with Syd and ditched Taz because of *Shira?*" Tweety shook her head sadly, her black-brown eyebrows knitting together in sympathy. "Poor Skye!"

"I don't want a pity party." Tweety's sympathy was nice, but Skye needed a practical solution. She had enough self-pity to last a lifetime. "I want help! What should I do?"

A beat of silence passed in the steamy spa as each girl thought the question over. Skye stared miserably at the billows of white steam surrounding her. The air in here reminded her of Syd—cloying and dense.

"If *he* dumps *you*, Shira can't kick you out," offered Ophelia.

"Uh-huh," nodded Skye miserably. "I came to the same conclusion. But Syd is like a hungry puppy, and I have a porterhouse steak stuffed in every pocket."

"We can figure this out," said Ophelia firmly, sliding off her massage bench to come sit next to Skye. "Boys always hate me. How hard could it be?"

"Okay, got it!" chirped Tweety, grinning at Skye and Ophelia on the bench across from her. "Tell him he's kissing wrong. Guys *hate* to be bossed around."

"Can't," cried Skye. "He's too sensitive. He'll just do what I say, or cry."

Ophelia sat up straighter. "Keep talking about how cute his brothers are!"

"Can't. Too sensitive. See above."

"Shave your head!" yelled Tweety.

"Can't."

"Why not?"

"He thinks I'm beautiful no matter what."

Both Ophelia and Tweety gasp-gushed. "Aw!"

Then Tweety tried another angle. "Okay. What is he into? Other than you, I mean."

"Poetry." Skye rolled her eyes. She never wanted to hear

another poem as long as she lived. Syd had ruined the English language for her. "Romance. Crying."

"Okay, I've got it." Tweety jumped off her massage table and opened the door to the steam room. "You just need to be as un-poetic and un-dateable as possible."

Skye pictured the un-dateable girls she'd known back in Westchester. They'd had bad hygeine, bad grades, bad clothes, or bad attitudes. Skye nodded. She could become un-dateable. She just had to be as ugly and hateful, inside and out.

"Tweety, you're a genius!" Skye grabbed her spare towel and smiled as she wrapped it around her head, already coming up with gross ideas for her new un-dateable alter ego.

As she followed Ophelia and Tweety down the pink leather-lined hallway to the locker room, Skye's mind relaxed along with her limbs.

Half an hour later, the three dancers stepped out of the Pavilion and into the still-bright late afternoon. Skye squint-smiled at her two companions. "Operation Gross-Syd-Out starts now." She winked and high-kicked a sandaled foot gracefully in the air.

"Good, because here he comes," Ophelia whispered, chin-thrusting toward the gravel path in front of them.

"Hey," said Syd, shuffling toward them and clutching a

huge paper cup from the Alphas café. Skye fake-smiled at him, wishing for the millionth time that he had as much edge as his clothes did. His navy Alphas blazer looked like he'd run over it with a lawnmower, and dozens of safety pins sat clustered on his shoulders like punk epaulettes. Under the blazer, he wore a vintage Def Leppard T-shirt. "How was the spa?" His angular face crumpled into an eager smile, exposing the tiny gap between his two front teeth. His green eyes were stuck to Skye's face like a set of cheap false eyelashes.

"Great," Skye muttered, shooting a half-guilty smirk at Ophie.

"For my superstar." Syd's deep, gravelly voice didn't match the cloying words he spoke, but his beaming smile did. He thrust the sweating cup into Skye's hands. "I got you a strawberry-banana smoothie to rehydrate."

Here goes nothing, Skye thought, channeling Milly Vanderhooven from back in Westchester. Milly spoke exclusively in acronyms and loved discussing her digestive tract.

She smiled at Syd, her teal eyes meeting his green ones "OMG, TY!"

She wrapped her glossed lips around the straw, took a huge gulp of the smoothie, and then forced a burp, praying Taz wasn't lurking anywhere nearby. Then she snort-giggled and snuck a look at Syd, who seemed unfazed. Tweety and

Ophelia covered their mouths, both girls struggling not to burst out laughing.

Skye studied Syd's face for a reaction. *Nada!* His green eyes still shone with Skye-appreciation. "Nice one, babe. Once, I burped an entire Fugazi song."

Skye needed to turn up her gross-o-meter, fast.

"Ew, my burp smells like salami!" Skye screech-giggled, fanning the air in front of her face with her hand. "OMG, Syd, tell me there isn't salami in my smoothie!" She burped again, for good measure.

This time Syd's thick eyebrows furrowed like kissing caterpillars and his full lips twisted into a grimace. Surely he was grossed out enough by his burping belle to take off running? Skye crossed her fingers on her right hand and held them behind her back.

"Is something wrong?" Skye grinned at him, practically tasting her freedom underneath her nasty burp.

"I'm going to talk to the chef ASAP. They need to make another one of these, or check the blender, or something. I'll catch up with you later."

"Wait, Syd!" Skye tried, but he'd already broken into a jog and was headed straight for the café. She stared at his skinny jeans disappearing back into the Pavilion, her mouth hanging open in a bewildered O.

"Let's ditch him in the cafeteria," sighed Skye. "I need to think. And to think, I need to walk."

"This is going to be tougher than we thought." Ophelia frowned and threw her arm around Skye's slumped shoulders. "But at least you got rid of him for now."

Skye shook her head dejectedly, spraying a few water droplets from her damp hair onto her shoulders. "Yeah, but he'll be back."

Like salami, Syd couldn't be kept down for long.

8

ALPHA INFIRMARY
PANACEA SUITE
TUESDAY, SEPTEMBER 28TH
7:02 A.M.

Allie pressed the CALL button on the clear screen hovering in front of her, and Madame Vandertramp, her scarf-draped French teacher, went instantly mute on the video screen. Allie watched as Madame stabbed a whiteboard with her glamorous French-manicured fingers and silently explained the importance of *verbes reflexives*.

"How can we help?" a melodic, health-promoting voice chirped from the screen.

"Um, could I have another pillow? And maybe some more soup?" Allie modulated her voice to sound pinched with a sinus infection.

"Right away, Allie. Some tea to go with it?"

"Sure," Allie fake-coughed. "Thanks." She pushed the CLASS button and was right back to French, having barely missed a thing. But her eyes drifted to the wall of her room, where a vertical waterfall burbled soothingly. Every few

51

minutes, the waterfall was tinted a different color. Right now, it was purple. Allie smiled, leaned back into her 1,000-thread-count sheets, and decided she'd have to fake sick for at least a week—the Alpha Infirmary was more relaxing than a five-star hotel.

Nurse Nightengale, the infirmary's efficient chief, appeared silently, wearing a white lab coat cinched in the middle by a white leather belt decorated with a red patent leather cross. She smiled, her brow creased in an empathetic worry-line that made Allie feel as protected as if it were her own mother's face hovering above her bed in Santa Ana.

"How are we feeling?" Nurse Nightengale said softly.

"Not so good," she whispered, rubbing her glands on either side of her throat.

"Drink this," Nurse Nightengale said. "And just relax. If you feel too tired to attend your virtual classes, we have a video library with all the latest movies and TV shows you've been missing. Research shows that watching humorous programming can actually cure ailments, so this is the one place on the island where it's available."

Ohmuhgud, rom-coms! Allie's fingers twitched in a Pavlovian response to her drug of choice, but she hid her hands under the covers and tried not to smile. She forced her head to nod slowly, hiding her excitement.

"I . . . I think I need to just lie here for a while and try to eat and sleep."

"Of course, you do that. And just let me know if there's anything else I can bring you." With that, Nurse Nightengale's clogs clomped out of the room, as she shut Allie's door behind her.

Allie brought the soup spoon to her lips and smile-swallowed. The sick-meals here made her mother's toast and ginger ale routine seem like prison food. The chamomile hibiscus tea tasted like it had been plucked straight from the tree. If you couldn't get well and forget your problems here, Allie thought, you couldn't be happy anywhere. Allie pushed another pillow behind her back and stretched out in bed, enjoying the feel of the temp-adjust sheets warming the soles of her feet and the knobby joints of her knees. It was so comfortable in this hospital that she could almost forget about Darwin rejecting her in the garden last night. Almost. She bit her lower lip hard enough to wince and squeezed her eyes shut, wondering how long she'd be able to hide out here.

"Pssst! Allie!"

Allie opened one navy blue eye and turned to the room's window, where a set of twinkling brown eyes blinked back at her.

"Charlie!"

Charlie waved her over to the window and mimed opening it. "I brought you something."

Charlie was such a good friend! Who else would bother

to track her down here? Allie jumped out of bed, wrapping her shiny oyster-colored robe around her narrow waist, and rushed over to the huge window.

"You sure you don't want to just come in the regular way? It's an infirmary, not a jail."

Charlie grinned up at her. "Nah. This is way more *NCIS*."

Allie yanked harder and slid the huge pane of glass up. She hoisted Charlie through the window, both girls giggle-grunting as they toppled onto the floor.

"Um, Al?" Charlie said, once they were in the room together. "Are you even sick? I'm getting a pretty healthy vibe here." Charlie pulled Allie up off the floor and pulled up a chair next to Allie's bed.

"I'm *emotionally* sick," Allie whined, flopping back into bed and pulling the covers up to her chin. "I needed a place to heal from my Darwin-inflicted wounds." She lay back and sigh-stared at the ceiling, sneaking a peek at Charlie when her friend didn't answer.

Charlie crossed her legs, and then uncrossed them. Then crossed them in the other direction. She looked preoccupied, and her eyes darted around the posh hospital room before they landed back on Allie. But before Allie could ask what was up, the doorknob turned, followed by a sharp double-knock on the door. "Allie, may I come in? I brought you some Tylenol," Nurse Nightengale's soothing voice called.

"Sure, of course," Allie coughed, back in sick-Alpha mode. She immediately fell back on her pillows, grabbed a fistful of tissues, and blew her nose as the nurse walked back into the room.

"Take two," the nurse said, nodding curtly at Charlie and handing Allie two silver tablets.

"Dank you, Durse," Allie sigh-groaned, feeling her eyes turn watery and the color in her face drain out until she was a sickly shade of eggshell. Faking sick had always been something Allie was good at, ever since Jordan Janowitz had pushed her face into the sand in third-grade recess and she needed a mental-health day to plot her revenge.

"Feel better, Allie," Nurse Nightengale replied soothingly, leaning over her and swiping a credit card–sized thermometer over Allie's forehead. "You have a slight fever. One oh one point one. Make sure your friend doesn't stay too long."

"Sure," Allie said, willing her sweat ducts to open up on her forehead and release a hint of clammy exhaustion. "She's just telling me about our homework for, um, a project we're doing."

Once Nurse Nightengale slid Allie's door shut, she resumed her discussion with Charlie.

"So anyway, yeah. I'm emotionally ill. I threw myself at Darwin and he rejected me. Not to mention that AJ sings these vicious songs about me, and everyone else in school except you and Skye still thinks I'm a psycho identity thief who deserves to be avoided like the plague."

"But you're about to hit your stride. All of this will just make you stronger!" Charlie smoothed out a wrinkle in her pleated mini and furrowed her brow emphatically.

"No, all of this would make *you* stronger," Allie said, her voice wavering. She sat up and looked Charlie in the eye. "I'm not like you, Charlie. I'm not a real Alpha. I don't have a real talent, or any idea of what it could be. It's different for you. You go into that lab and you know exactly what you're doing. I have no idea what I'm doing here. And without Darwin, I have no purpose—"

Just then, the door to her room opened, interrupting Allie and Charlie yet again. *Seriousleh, can't they let a girl recuperate?* But she reasoned that it wouldn't be the Alpha Island infirmary unless they pulled out all the stops.

"Knock knock, Allie," Nurse Nightengale said, the mole on her chin wobbling as she talked. "I brought you a cool compress with juniper and begonia essence. Proven to reduce fever."

Allie took the pink washcloth, monogrammed with two A's in darker pink script, and fell back on her pillow. She whispered a tortured "thanks" before slapping the cloth onto her forehead and shutting her eyes.

"I'm going soon, I promise," she heard Charlie say to the nurse.

When her door slid shut again, Allie continued.

"So for now, this is where I belong. In hiding. If I can't be an Alpha at least I can do a great job of faking sick."

"Faking sick is no way to get over . . ." Charlie stopped mid-rant and stared at Allie like she was her own personal science experiment. "Wait a second. Your performance in here, in front of the nurse! It's Oscar-worthy, Allie. You've been sitting on this huge talent and calling it *faking*."

"Faking is a *talent?*"

"Yeah," Charlie laughed. "It is. It's called *acting*."

Allie ran an unsure hand through her honey-blond hair. *Acting?* She'd always been a good fake—she was great at faking being AJ, until the real AJ showed up and ruined it. She was great at faking deafness when AJ sang her crappy songs about her. She'd faked Cream of Wheat tasting good when she'd posed as a model for a supermarket coupon spread. And when she was ten, she'd done such a good job of faking sadness over the death of Sir Swimmy, her gold-fish, that her father had gone out and bought her a kitten. Then she'd faked being allergic to Sizzles the kitten so she wouldn't have to change his litter box.

"Maybe you're right," she conceded. "They are pretty much the same thing."

"Of course I'm right." Charlie grinned. "And I have a way to put your acting skills to use."

"How?" asked Allie.

"I brought you this," Charlie said, reaching into her bra. She rolled her brown eyes toward the ceiling as she pulled out a glossy page of a magazine that had been folded to the size of a stick of gum. "It's from Italian *Vogue*." Charlie passed it to Allie.

"You want me to fake being Kate Moss in Italy?" Allie unfolded it slowly, careful not to rip the glossy paper.

"Just open it," Charlie said.

Gently smoothing out the paper on her rolling hospital tray, Allie sucked in her breath. *Adorable!* It was Darwin's older brother, the blond and chiseled Melbourne, posing in an ad for an Italian denim company called Cara Mio. In the black-and-white picture, Melbourne was shirtless and leaning up against a wall, eyeing a miniskirted girl who was halfway out of the frame.

"Nice six-pack. Nice jaw. Good angles. Hot ad," Allie murmured, studying the picture with the eye of a former model. Allie had to admit, Mel was more crushable than cardboard. If her heart hadn't already been bulldozed by one of the Brazille Boys, she might have jumped on the bandwagon.

"It's Mel!" Charlie exclaimed, as though the fact weren't obvious.

"I *know* it's Mel," said Allie, struggling to keep irritation out of her voice. "But what does this have to do with me?"

"I know you're not over Darwin," Charlie said patiently. "But Mel is a mega-hawttie, and he's single, and I think you two might have a lot in common. If nothing else, he'd be a distraction. One that's healthier than"—she waved her hand dismissively around the room—"than pretending to be so unhealthy!"

"No thanks," she said, shaking her head so her blond waves smacked her pillow. "I can't just shut my feelings for Darwin off and turn on a crush on Mel. I'm not a fuse box!" She squinted her lash-fringed eyes at Charlie, wishing her aPod could read a person's motives and not just their bio. How could Allie be sure Charlie's intentions were pure? What if Charlie wanted to get back together with Darwin? They used to be soul mates—wasn't it possible that Charlie decided she wanted him back? "You're not . . . just doing this to get back together with Darwin, are you? If you like him, just be honest and tell me."

Charlie recoiled in her chair, sitting back so fast it looked like she'd been punched by an invisible hand. Her cheeks reddened and she studied the tiles of the infirmary floor as if searching for what to say.

"I-I-I know you're not a fuse box," Charlie finally stammered, looking up from the floor and grabbing Allie's hand. "And I don't want Darwin back. I just want you to be happy. Will you go out with Mel once, just to see? If nothing else, you can practice your acting and get some of your self-confidence back. And it *might* make Darwin jealous enough to realize what he's giving up."

Allie breathed out a gushing sigh. If going out with Mel could get Darwin to like her again, maybe Charlie's idea was worth considering. And the possibility of gaining some notoriety at the Academy for something other than impersonating Allie J was hard to resist. There was no point in trying to erase her feelings for Darwin by dating his brother, but maybe Charlie was right. Maybe hanging with a guy who actually liked her would be a good feeling? Allie had her doubts, but she shrugged them off like an ill-fitting trench.

"How do we make this happen?"

Allie nodded and listened as Charlie sketched the outlines of a plan for meeting up with Mel, acting excited as she went on. And on. Because, Allie told herself, that's what actors do. They act.

9

"Are we there yet?" Skye asked miserably. Her stomach lurched as the A-shaped air-chair she shared with Charlie and Allie swayed in high-altitude wind, hoisting the three Jackie O's up Mount Olympus, the tallest landmass on Alpha Island. Fifty feet below the chairlift she could see the tops of pine trees shivering, mirroring her own trembling nerves. If today's assault on Syd's senses didn't work, she might have to join Allie in the infirmary for fear of a nervous collapse.

"Smell that mountain freshness," Allie shouted into the wind, taking a big gulp of pine-scented, snow-cooled air. "Reminds me of the ski slopes in Tahoe!"

"Reminds me of an out-of-control roller coaster run by drunk carnies," mumbled Skye, unzipping her gunmetal gray parka halfway. The breeze-battered chairlift was just like her life right now—out of her control. But looking across the air-chair at her fellow O's, the same could be said

61

about them, too. Charlie had been nervous, jumpy, and clumsy all morning, and Allie was weirdly chipper for no discernable reason—almost manically so. In her gold belted puffer and matching gold fleece headband wrapped around her honeyed hair, Allie reminded Skye of an Austrian ski champion. Charlie looked cute, too, in an optic white parka that offset her mahogany hair, but she had chewed her nails down to the quick. Her forehead was creased with worry.

Skye clutched the safety bar on the chairlift and leaned forward, scanning the ground for Alpha girls. The competition to land the Brazille brothers was so fierce among the eighty-eight Alphas that Charlie had decided to leak fake locations for their picnic to throw girls off the scent. Down by the beach, Skye spotted fifteen girls in glittery bikinis, standing around sniffing the air for testosterone.

"I can almost see the burn lines from here," Skye said, pointing at the beach and wondering which Brazille bro they were waiting for.

"I hope they don't find out Darwin was with us today," Charlie sigh-nodded. Down at the foot of Mount Olympus, at the Academy's riding stables, three girls dressed in breeches and boots were hitting one another angrily with riding crops. "And it looks like Shelly Yip, Britney Saperstein, and Nuala Lapore realized Mel isn't showing up for that trail ride. Oops."

All week, Alphas had been driven to desperate acts in

the hope of impressing a Brazille Boy. It was like an episode of *The Bachelor* and *24* combined. So far, Skye had heard about a broken ankle (Jeanette Hollis, trampled by a pack of girls running after Dingo near the Arts Building) and more sabotage than on an episode of *America's Next Top Model*. Tales were circulating of bleach in shampoo bottles, Sharpie ink in toothpaste, garlic oil in perfume bottles.

But nobody had been sabotaged as much as Skye had sabotaged herself. In her quest to gross Syd out, she'd gone from a toned ten to a grungy, greasy, ill-tempered two. Still, Syd clung to her like toilet paper on a shoe. But that was all about to change, hopefully, and maybe she would get another chance at . . . *ohmuhgud.*

Skye craned her neck to get a better view of the *Joan of Arc,* Shira's yacht in the middle of Lake Alpha. Standing on the deck was a tiny, ant-sized Taz, squeezing sunscreen onto his hands, surrounded by a pack of bathing suit–clad Alphas.

"Sorry, babe." Charlie flashed Skye a sympathetic smile. "Taz could never resist a party. But someday soon, you two will put Syd behind you. I think Taz liked you more than he's ever liked any one girl before."

"Until I ruined it!" Skye moaned, reaching a dirt-encrusted fingernail inside the greasy tangle of hair. "My life is hell. My only hope is that today, Syd will realize that if he sticks with me, his life will be hell, too."

"I thought your life was *smell*," joked Allie.

Skye nodded, chewing her lip. Allie was right—Skye had finally achieved maximum nastiness. To be any grosser, she would have to contract a case of scabies along with gingivitis, both of which were too icky to contemplate. "Yeah, today is as gross as I get. Which reminds me," Skye dug through the picnic basket at the girls' feet. "I packed a snack."

Skye fished out a yellow onion and began to peel off the skin, her stomach recoiling at the thought of what she was about to do.

Allie's eyes widened with alarm. "Skye, you are *not* going to eat that."

"I have to!" Skye snapped. "This is my last hope! If Syd leans in for a kiss and smells this, maybe he'll reconsider our undying love." She pinched her nostrils shut with two fingers and bit into the onion as if it were an apple, chewing it miserably as tears streamed down her face. Her gag reflex kicked in and she fought through it to swallow a mouthful of raw onion.

"Nice touch," Charlie giggle-grimaced, gesturing toward Skye's jaw line, where an eruption of chin-zits now dotted her otherwise flawless complexion.

"Lip liner," Skye gag-grinned, shrugging as she tossed the half-eaten onion overboard into the pine forest. "Triple's idea."

As the air-chair skidded toward the clearing at the top of the mountain, the girls zipped up their parkas, applied Purell (Allie), chewed her cuticles inscrutably (Charlie), and dusted faux dandruff made of cornstarch and cookie crumbs across her shoulders (Skye).

"What's my motivation again?" Allie sat up straighter and adjusted her ski headband, channeling her new budding-actress persona as she grilled Charlie.

Charlie let out a tiny sigh and shot a quick look at Skye before launching into a pep talk. Evidently, Allie was about to set into motion the performance of a lifetime. "You're pretending you're over Darwin, and into Mel. Act confident, cool, and totally in control. That way, Darwin will see what he's missing and Mel will fall for you, which, with any luck, might make Darwin want you that much more."

Skye swallowed a bitter laugh. If there was one thing she'd learned while trying to shake Syd, it was that people never responded how you hoped they would.

Charlie paused, taking a breath and leaning over to scan the clearing for signs of the guys. "Best-case scenario," she continued, "you'll have *two* Brazille brothers fighting over you."

Allie nodded and chewed her lip in concentration as she whispered "cool, calm, confident" to herself as if preparing to walk onstage for Hollywood week on *American Idol*.

"Good luck, Al," Skye said. "May *one* of us make a love connection today, and may it not be me."

Skye narrowed her aquamarine eyes at the group of boys waiting for them. Syd stood next to the lift clutching a huge bunch of yellow and pink-flecked branches. Behind the flowers, his smile was as all-consuming as a black hole.

But as the air-chair slid in for a landing, Skye found Charlie's optimism infectious. After all, if Allie could act her way into Mel's heart, why couldn't Skye act her way out of Syd's? With any luck, Skye would be single by dinner, and she could wash that man—and a week of filth—right out of her hair.

10

As the air-chair dipped in for a landing, Charlie gritted her teeth and hoped the hamster-wheel of nerves in her stomach would slow to a halt soon. She snuck a peek at Allie's serene-looking face and hoped for the millionth time that her crazy plan would work: that Mel would fall for Allie, and that in time, Allie would be so wrapped up with Mel that she wouldn't be able to remember Darwin's name. And most of all, that she would come out of this high-altitude triple date without making any enemies. She glanced across from her at Skye, who looked as bad as Charlie felt. If Syd was as grossed out by Skye as Charlie was, soon all the Jackie O's would have what they wanted.

"There they are," whispered Allie, a slow smile creeping across her glossed lips. She looked confident and radiated calm.

"Picnic time," Charlie sing-songed lamely. She was way

too nervous to eat anything, but the mountaintop would make a great romantic backdrop for Allie and Mel's first date.

Just as they were about to jump off the lift, Allie reached over and grabbed Charlie's hand in hers and squeezed it hard. Suddenly it was as though the real Allie jumped out of actress-Allie's exterior and flashed Charlie a wild-eyed look. "Are you sure you're over Darwin? Something still feels weird about this."

No, I'm not sure at all!

"Of course," lied Charlie, praying her voice wouldn't shake. "I want this to work more than anyone." Charlie did want this to work, and by *this*, she meant the Mel-Allie connection.

The air-chair touched down for a moment and Charlie grabbed Allie and Skye's hands as they all jumped off. Charlie waved at the boys, who stood near a stand of pines on three sides of a huge picnic blanket, and said an internal prayer that Allie wouldn't find out what she was up to, that Mel would be all over Allie like blue on a Na'vi, and that Darwin would forgive her someday for making him lie. It was a lot to ask, but Charlie would find a way to repay the universe if she got what she wanted. She was an Alpha Inventor, wasn't she? Maybe she'd cure cancer. At the very least, she would cure Allie's broken heart. And, if all went well, Charlie would also mend her own.

A few minutes later the three Jackie O's trudged toward the immense picnic blanket, each nervous for her own reasons.

"This is ah-mazing." Charlie couldn't help marveling over the spread.

Darwin was a serial DIY-er, hating to let others do what he could do himself, and this picnic had his trademark favorites all over it. There were three kinds of everything: fresh-squeezed fruit juice (pear-pomegranate, grapefruit-guava, and ginger lemonade), flatbread pizzas (rosemary portobello, tomato basil, and chicken apple sausage), and three cakes (flourless chocolate, lemon mousse, and strawberry shortcake).

"Wow," breathed Allie, wiping tears of shock-appreciation from her eyes. She smiled sweetly at Darwin as he sat down on the blanket, then shot a furtive glance at Melbourne, who looked ready for his close-up as he leaned against a nearby pine tree. "I didn't know guys could do stuff like this," she said to the whole group.

"We're not your average guys." Mel's lavender eyes twinkled as he flashed a smile, highlighting his strong jaw and cleft chin. He wore forest green snowboarding pants with a white down jacket. His straight blond hair matched Allie's newly restored locks. "It might not be the food court at the mall, but we came close."

"I love mall food," Allie sighed wistfully, as if remembering a beloved old friend.

"Me too," said Mel. "There's something about Sbarro, Starbucks, and the scent of new clothes that feels so right."

Charlie smiled as she watched Allie sizing up Mel.

Crush, activated!

"Have you seen the view from up here?" Mel asked Allie in a smooth voice. "There's a lookout point a few yards that way."

Allie winked one navy blue eye at Charlie before breezily following Mel. "So where do you shop?" Charlie heard her asking as they disappeared behind a stand of pines.

Careful not to get too close to Darwin lest she inhale the smell of his cinnamon-scented toothpick, Charlie walked toward Syd and Skye on the far side of the clearing.

"And now, allow me to woo you," Syd was saying, brandishing a slim volume of Emily Dickinson poetry. His moss-green eyes gazed at Skye like he was an island castaway and she was a case of Aquafina.

Skye grabbed the book out of his hands, grinning at Charlie and wiggling her eyebrows significantly. "How about I read it to *you*, Pooky," she said, reaching up to scratch her scalp under her greasy blond dreadlocks.

"Of course, my love," said Syd, his angular face stretched into an adoring smile. "Page sixty-four is the one I was going—"

"Got it, Pookers," Skye snapped, turning to the page he'd bookmarked and clearing her throat. She raised the book to cover her face and pulled a scallion out of her parka pocket, shoving it in her mouth and chewing it up.

Ew! Charlie cringed on Syd's behalf. Watching Skye and Syd was like watching *American Idol* auditions. You didn't really want to see it, but you couldn't look away.

Skye leaned toward Syd, nuzzling her face in his shoulder, and began to recite the poetry in her breathiest voice: "Hope is the thing with feathers, that perches in the soul, And sings the tune without the words, and never stops at all."

Syd sniffed the air as Skye read. His eyes were suddenly pink and watery.

"What's wrong, Pookers McGookers?" Skye asked, her voice dripping with faux-concern.

"I'm sort of stuffed up today," Syd said. "I can't smell a thing, not even your delicious Aveda shampoo."

Skye slapped her forehead and moaned in defeat.

"It's okay, babe, it's just a little cold. I'll get well quick, I promise," Syd's bee-stung lips formed a reassuring smile and his gray-green eyes glittered.

Charlie couldn't bear to hear any more. She spun around and sat down a few feet away from Darwin, careful not to get too close. Her eyes caught his and he grimace-grinned at her through clenched yet adorably white teeth. *Pretend you don't like him*, Charlie reminded herself, quickly staring down at the plaid picnic blanket. "This is so nice, Dar—"

"Just tell me how long I have to keep this up," he hiss-smiled.

"As long as it takes for Allie to realize Mel and she might

71

be soul mates!" Charlie snapped. Didn't he know she was doing this for *him*?

Charlie met Allie's gaze and she giddily beckoned Charlie over, waving her flame-red fingertips toward her chest. "Charlie, you need to see this view!"

"On my way." Charlie jumped up, brushing a few rose petals off her butt before jogging over to Allie. Meanwhile, Mel strode back to the picnic with a pleased look on his face. "Spill it," she commanded when she reached Allie.

"You were right, Mel is ah-mazing, and I can already feel my confidence making a comeback." Allie smiled wide, her eyes crinkling with genuine happiness.

Charlie's spirits soared higher than the tops of the snow-capped evergreens surrounding them. Now that Allie liked Mel, she would forget all about Darwin. When that happened, Charlie could get back together with him without disturbing the peace at Jackie O.

"So? Did Darwin seem jealous while I was gone?" Allie's voice broke through Charlie's daydream and brought her back to earth.

Oh.

"Uh . . . maybe? I'm not sure." Charlie reached down and wiped some mud from the tops of her gold boots. She needed to put this conversation in reverse and get Allie back onto the right BB. "Mel and you will make such a gorgeous couple. You guys could model together!"

"It'll never work." Allie shook her head, setting a honey-blond wave loose from her headband. She widened her navy blue eyes and gave Charlie a stern look. "Actors and models are destined to fight for the spotlight. Now that I'm serious-leh pursuing acting, I need a down-to-earth guy like Darwin more than ever." Allie blinked her thick black lashes emphatically, but when Charlie didn't say anything, her blue eyes narrowed. "Are you sure you're not falling for Darwin again?"

"I told you, no!" Charlie snapped. "I'm here for *you*. Not *me*."

"Good. Then find out if he's jealous, would you? Acting like I'm interested in Mel is my most challenging role yet!" Allie smiled, then turned toward the picnic to continue her performance.

Charlie swallowed hard, wishing she could yell *cut* and put an end to the sordid scene. Her comedy of manners was quickly turning into a tragedy of epic proportions.

11

Allie ran a shaking hand nervously across her blow-out, smoothing out flyaways and nerves. She was late for her first acting class. She hadn't felt this anxious or intimidated since she'd had her first head shots taken at the Barbizon Modeling School in the Santa Ana mall. Her eyes widened as she stepped onto the plush red carpet that extended like a rectangular tongue from the giant gold façade of the Performing Arts complex. The entrance to the building was a depressingly tragic frown, which didn't help Allie's mood. Thankfully when the doors whooshed open, the frown curled into a laughing smile.

Inside, three gorgeous SITs (Stars In Training) walked toward her, each of them dressed like extras from *Oliver Twist*, their tweed vests and kneesocks smudged with soot. They reminded Allie of Mary-Kate Olsen on a bad day— homeless-looking, but beautiful.

74

"Wot's *she* doin' 'ere?" one of the girls snort-snickered, turning to her sooty pals.

Another one rolled her eyes, then quickly reassumed her street urchin character study, adjusting a straw hat that rode jauntily atop a mass of kinky black curls. "I 'aven't a clue— must be an impostor convention!"

The three pseudo-British urchins laughed as Allie's face turned the color of the carpet beneath her. *It's true. Identity theft doesn't make me an actress. It makes me a criminal.* She shame-stared straight ahead and stalked past them and through the entrance, Purelling even though (she hoped!) she hadn't touched them.

Finally, she arrived at her class in the amphitheater. The huge room consisted of a giant round stage surrounded by rows of chairs—there were at least five hundred empty seats. Allie shivered at the thought of all of them being filled with a huge audience.

Her eyes scanned the scene, watching as holographic sets on the stage dissolved and re-appeared every few seconds. Quotes from great actors and directors and famous lines from movies and plays illuminated the walls like glowing neon caterpillars. The teacher of the class was a woman rounder than Humpty Dumpty with hair dyed a shade of red so bright it was nearly neon. She was dressed in head-to-toe black, and her lips were an even brighter shade of tomato red than her hair. But Big Red had it. *It* being that hard-todefine quality known as charisma, animal magnetism, star power. Her chubby chin jiggled as she walked and talked. Still, Allie was totally entranced by her.

Allie's trance was so deep that she nearly screamed when a finger silently tapped her on the shoulder. Allie's navy blue eyes made contact with Triple Threat's catlike golden ones, which were narrowed quizzically.

"You're in this class?" Allie whispered through clenched teeth, not wanting to unfreeze and incur the wrath of Big Red.

"Uh-huh," smirked Triple, arching one perfectly plucked eyebrow. "I *own* this class."

Two sharp hand-claps bounced their attention back to the acting teacher. "New York subway!" the teacher yelled. "*Hear* the rumbling along the track! *Feel* the stress of being sandwiched underground! *Smell* the unappetizing smells!"

Some of the girls refroze in new positions as subway riders, hanging on invisible poles or sitting on invisible subway seats, their faces contorting into masks of tension and their bodies jiggling as if being rocked by a moving train, while others took the opportunity to create characters. Sunita Sanchez, who Allie knew from French class, morphed into a homeless person and walked around asking for spare change, jingling an invisible cup of coins. Another girl rolled her eyes and pretended to block her out with a giant newspaper.

As Sunita approached her, Allie quickly stuck her nose into her shirt to block out her imaginary homeless-person germs and concentrated on not gagging on the imaginary smell of pee permeating their subway car. Before she knew it, she'd fished out her bottle of Purell and slathered both hands in it, instantly feeling more protected.

Big Red stopped her monologue and walked over to Allie. "Good improv for your first time. Nice germophobia! You must be the IT. I'm Careen."

Allie smiled nervously, confused by Careen's acronym. *Is IT an acting term?* Her mind groped at the possibilities: Improv Trainee? Interpreter of Theater? I Thespian? Careen stood a bit too close to Allie, her chunky arms folded. She seemed to want a response.

"IT?" Allie finally squeaked.

"Identity Thief."

"Oh." Tears instantly sprang to Allie's deep blue eyes and her nervous smile vanished. Allie wished she could vanish along with it.

But then Careen's high-pitched laugh filled Allie's ears, sounding like the yapping of two tiny dogs stuffed into a purse. She smacked Allie on the back with a meaty, ring-covered hand, hard enough that Allie bumped into Triple. "In this class, IT is a compliment! I heard all about the scandal," Careen paused, taking a wheezing breath, "and I'm elated to work with someone with such *enormous* ambition.

What a brilliant way to get into the Academy!"

Careen gushed. Allie blushed.

The redhead circled Allie like a bargain hunter eyeing the clearance rack. "That kind of hunger cannot be taught."

Careen bulldozed her way through the imaginary subway car. "Check out the bios of these fame-seekers on your aPod later. You'll see they've all gone to great lengths to be here. You're no different than they are; you just took a different path. You are home now, my future ingénue. Welcome!"

Careen came charging back toward Allie, her arms outstretched. Allie took a breath as Careen grabbed her shoulders and pressed her face to her ample bosom in a suffocating-yet-nurturing hug.

Lost in the black fabric of Careen's chest, Allie's emotions took her by surprise. Finally, someone was being nice to Allie! Someone thought she belonged. Hot tears prickled at her eyes.

When Careen finally let her go, Allie noticed she'd left a big wet spot on her teacher's left boob.

"Remember this feeling, Allie. Use it in your craft." Careen's lipsticky teeth flashed Allie another smile. "Now, let's get you up to speed."

Careen explained that this was an acting warm-up exercise. The idea was to mime whatever she called out. "Don't *think*!" Careen screeched. "React! Leave yourself and your thoughts behind and *become*."

A surge of hopeful relief coursed through Allie's veins. She wanted nothing more than to leave herself behind forever. She joined the girls on their invisible subway, some of whom peered at her over their invisible newspapers in a disinterested way, just like real commuters.

Allie grabbed on to an invisible pole and started the ride. Then Careen clapped her hands again. "Electric shock!"

The actors-in-training began shaking spastically, their limbs flying as if they'd been hurled against an electric fence. But the word *shock* meant one thing and one thing only to Allie. Shock was finding her ex-boyfriend Fletcher kissing her ex-best friend Trina on the *Finding Nemo* ride at Disneyland. So she channeled that shock. Her eyes bulged. Her mouth hung open, forming a horrified black hole. Tears began to fall from her eyes again, this time because she had just been betrayed by the two people she loved most. No electricity required.

Careen clapped again, but this time the applause was for Allie. "Nice, Allie. Subtle, elegant work. Class, please follow Allie's lead. Shock isn't just something we get from hair dryers."

Allie's memory of Fletcher and Trina was replaced by elation. She pushed her shoulders back and stuck out her B-cups, reveling in an emotion she'd nearly forgotten existed: *pride*. She gloat-grinned at Triple, who had stopped writhing on the floor to stare at Allie, naked jealousy radiating from her golden irises.

Careen clapped again, pulling Allie back to the stage and her acting ambitions. "Revenge!"

Allie imagined sitting at the Oscars in a Zac Posen off-the-shoulder gown, her earlobes dripping with diamonds and emeralds. She looked over and smiled at Darwin sitting next to her, handsome in a tux, squeezing her hand as Natalie Portman announced the winner for Best Actress. "Allie A. Abbott!"

Allie pictured her tearful acceptance speech and zoomed out in her imagination to include Fletcher sitting in his parents' basement rec room, in the dark, alone, watching her on TV. A single tear rolled down Fletcher's cheek.

Maybe, just maybe, acting would give Allie back everything Fletcher had taken away—starting with her self-respect.

12

CENTER FOR THE ARTS
THEATER OF DIONYSUS
MONDAY, OCTOBER 4TH
4:49 P.M.

The clear walls of the dance studio—an all-glass cube dangling fifty feet above the tree line like dice on the island's rearview mirror—dripped with condensation. After two hours of rehearsal, the dance cube was hotter than a Bikram yoga class.

Inside, Skye stood with her back arched, a sheen of sweat covering her strong limbs and making them blend in with her shiny silver boyshorts and dance cami. Breathing hard, she tensed in preparation for her solo, every molecule in her body vibrating along with Lady Gaga's "Bad Romance." Skye locked her elbows and watched through ten splayed fingers as Triple and Prue launched into perfectly synchronized back handsprings when Lady Gaga hit the second chorus. Next to her, Ophelia readied her flexed legs to race into the mix. Skye shot a quick glance at Mimi, who stood in front of them in a black Capezio halter dress, tango shoes, and thirty bangles jingling on each arm, yelling "ONE TWO THREE FOUR!" Pushing her B-cups out and waiting for her cue, Skye felt a giddy warmth, a delicious knowledge coursing through her veins, almost as good as a first kiss, or the first bite of food when you were really hungry: she was *back*, and she was *good*.

For the past two weekends and every night between, Skye had been working this routine. Like the Energizer Bunny, she kept going and going, even when everyone else was asleep or enjoying much-needed downtime. And now, Skye had done the routine so many times that she was on autopilot. Her senses weren't dulled, though—far from it. The dance was etched so deeply into her muscle memory that she didn't have to think—she simply flipped the switch and her body took over. The routine was as automatic as brushing her teeth, as tying her shoe, as flirting with a cute boy—or at least as automatic as flirting *used* to be, before Syd forced her to rewire that portion of her brain from *flirt* to *hurt*.

"Skye!" Mimi yelled, and Skye's attention snapped like a rubber band, flying back into the routine with the force of a ballistic missile. Her body followed her thoughts, leap-step-ball-changing onto center stage as four other dancers parted to make room for her. Her face locked into a fierce-yet-knowing grin, she began to pop and lock to the lyrics, her hips twitching like a robot doing the hula. As she slid onto the floor in a double split, she realized nobody could relate to the song more than she could. It was like Gaga had written it just for her.

I want your loving and I want your revenge
You and me could write a bad romance

As the other girls gathered around Skye to come in for the final moments of the routine, Skye's smile grew even bigger. She had nailed this. To the wall. With a nail gun.

"Pause," Mimi said to the voice-activated stereo, and Gaga instantly evaporated to nada. "Good work today, dancers. Andrea, as usual, you are owning the beat." Mimi's caramel features softened around a proud smile—on Mimi, a smile was almost as rare as the flowers on desert cacti that only bloomed once a year. Skye fought to keep her eyeballs from rolling in exasperation and swallowed a sigh. Her envious insides clenched as she waited for Mimi to torture her. And as if the cranky choreographer could read Skye's mind, Mimi locked her golden cat eyes, dramatically dusted with MAC Shimmer Smoothie shadow, with Skye's naked Tiffany box–blue ones. A half-smile flashed across her face. "Nice work, Sleeves. You've been practic-ing."

Skye blinked, too shocked to speak. Mimi sounded

almost . . . proud. "Thanks," she finally managed, afraid to say anything else for fear that Mimi would take back the compliment like it was a precious necklace—on loan for one night only.

Maybe all the drama with Syd had actually been a blessing, Skye thought, flexing and arching her feet. After all, the only reason she was so focused on practicing was so she wouldn't drown in the sticky pool of his saccharine-sweet adoration. Without Syd, Skye might still be at the top of Mimi's most-likely-to-suck list.

"Music, on!" Mimi clapped twice and put one hand on her muscled hip, her eyes scanning the room as the dancers sashayed into their positions and Gaga ushered the song in.

"And right, and left, and robot boogie!" yelled Mimi, bringing the group through their synchronized moves once again. Sandwiched between Ophelia and Tweety, Skye grinned with the joy of the dance, buoyed by the sensation of Triple dancing behind her, probably drilling a jealous hate-hole straight into her blond, bunned head.

Out of the corner of her eye, she noticed the elevator doors opening.

Blinking her concentration back to center stage, Skye tried to focus on an arm-windmill sequence, not wanting to let herself get distracted by whoever it might be.

"*Breathtaking*," someone whispered from across the room.

Uh-oh.

Of course it was Syd. Who else would be clueless enough to interrupt Mimi's class?

With his dark jeans ripped at the knee and his navy blazer covered on one side with rock 'n' roll pins, Syd looked half rocker-chic, half stalker-freak as he smiled at Skye.

Skye's glare stuck to him like a fresh blow-out to a MAC Lipglassed mouth. His gapped front teeth peeked out from under his deep-red lips, and as he waved, Skye noticed a small red envelope between his index and middle finger.

Skye's patience was already more frayed than the ankles of her oldest pair of J-Brands. She needed hand-delivered love notes from Syd the way Triple needed lessons in how to be annoying: not at all.

Skye attempted to subtly motion to him to GET AWAY, but she missed a crucial step, which put her in Tweety's line of movement. Suddenly, like a house of cards, all the dancers toppled, and Skye found herself on the bottom of a pileup of sweaty, Lycra'd limbs. She cringed as her fellow bun-heads fell one by one.

"Ooof! Ow! Ugh!"

Uh-oh. Skye struggled to breathe and to not burst into tears underneath Tweety, Prue, Ophelia, and the rest of the bun-heads.

"Ow," Tweety whimpered, rolling off of Skye and rubbing her slender hip.

"Not cool," moaned Prue, wrapping her light brown hair back into a high bun.

Skye staggered back onto her feet, her face burning with shame. "Sorry," she murmured. "My fault."

"Music, off! We're done for today," said Mimi, raising one eyebrow at Skye before turning away to make some adjustments to the holographic playback machine.

The girls dispersed, heading to the barre for a few cool-down stretches. As they sucked down spring water from their Alphas-emblazoned eco-friendly aluminum bottles, Skye refused to look in Syd's direction, joining Ophelia at the barre.

"Aren't you going to see what he wants?" Ophelia whispered, running a gold towel along her sweaty forehead.

Skye ignored her and threw her leg over the barre, leaning in for a deep quad stretch. Ophelia's hazel-green eyes moved from her to Syd and back again. Skye grunted as she pulled her leg off the bar, and when she threw her left foot up to stretch the other side, Ophelia turned to the wall, stuck her tongue out, and approximated a loud fart noise with her lips.

Tweety giggled, and Skye felt her face go crimson. Triple and Prue looked over and rolled their eyes. Then Skye let her eyes travel to Syd, who suddenly looked uncomfortable.

Ohmuhgud, maybe this will work!

"Again, Ophelia!" Skye whispered. "Keep 'em coming!"

As Skye went from first position to second, Ophelia let out a series of raspberries. "Ohmuhgud!" Skye shouted, covering her face as if she was mortified and hiding her smile in the process. "I shouldn't have had that burrito for lunch!" The bun-heads started laughing hysterically, and it was hard for Skye not to join them.

But this was life-or-death—she had to get Syd off her back before he caused her to break a limb.

Skye lunged into a grand plié and Ophelia let it rip again. Skye covered her mouth and opened her eyes wide, turning around to face Syd as the whole room erupted in laughter. But Syd wasn't laughing. His face had gone white with embarrassment, or nausea, or both. He began pushing the button on the elevator. Hard.

"How embarrassing!" Skye yelled merrily.

But Syd had stepped into the elevator, and for once his green eyes weren't glued to Skye. In fact, Skye was overjoyed to see that he looked desperate to get as far away from her as possible.

When the elevator doors closed, Skye high-fived Ophelia. "You are a genius!" she yelled.

"I have two older brothers." Ophelia shrugged. "Guess they taught me something."

Skye's spirits did a pirouette, rebounding after her mortifying maneuver during their last run-through. The prospect of being rid of Syd was a bigger relief than releasing a pent-up fart could ever be.

13

Charlie sighed with contentment in the passenger seat of Darwin's PAP (Personal Alpha Plane) as they floated higher in the sun-streaked sky. She pressed one hand against the cool glass of the curved window and gazed beneath them at the @-shaped island. To the west, the sun had begun its descent toward the horizon. It glowed a fiery orange as it hovered above the ocean, lighting up each building on the island in its wake. To the east, a brief spattering of rain had cleared only a few minutes ago, and a thin rainbow arched above the island like a silk ribbon decorating a wrapped gift.

This plane ride *was* a gift, Charlie mused as Darwin grinned at her and pulled the throttle on the PAP so the plane faced the rainbow. Darwin had been flying since he was twelve, and the ride was as smooth as foundation primer. Charlie looked around at the postcards Darwin had

89

taped up on the PAP's white leather interior—each place was somewhere they'd been together, and each one sparked a different, gooey-sweet memory. Belize, where they had swum with sea turtles. Rio, where they'd been in a parade during Carnival. Nova Scotia, where Darwin and Charlie had learned to pilot a sailboat. Iceland, where they'd eaten fermented shark and swum in steaming hot springs. Madagascar, where a monkey had stolen Darwin's guitar.

"Did you *plan* that?" Charlie whispered, pointing to the rainbow and half-believing that Darwin had, in fact, found a way to orchestrate the perfect combination of rain and sun. After all, he was a Brazille, which meant he had access to technology most people didn't even know existed yet.

"I'm good," Darwin said, flashing a half-smile and crinkling his gorgeous hazel eyes, "but I'm not *that* good. The universe just wants to entertain us, I guess."

"Guess so." They were doing a pretty good job of entertaining the universe, too, thought Charlie. She shivered as she recalled the dark cloud of hurt moving across Darwin's face as, one by one, she'd shot down four of his proposed meeting places (the beach? No way—too public! The Zen Garden? Uh-uh. Mount Olympus? Nixed. The yacht? Was he crazy?). She'd been the one to propose a ride in the PAP—it was the only place safe from prying eyes and picture-snapping aPods. Because no matter how badly Darwin wanted to be with her, Charlie just wasn't ready to go public. Not until the Allie mess was cleaned up, anyway.

"Girls must be throwing themselves at you left and right," said Charlie, trying to steer the conversation in a less romantic direction. "Now that Shira lifted the ban, you five are all anyone can think about."

"A little, I guess," said Darwin, running his finger along the touch-screen steering panel and sending the plane swooping beneath the rainbow. "I've gotten some texts. I just delete 'em. My brothers are having the time of their lives, though."

"What about Mel?" Charlie asked, hoping to keep her voice light. She didn't want Darwin to think she was desperate for Mel to hook up with Allie. He would see her desperation as controlling and manipulative instead of what it was—the only way for all four of them to be happy.

"He's into Allie, I think." Darwin stuck a cinnamon-scented toothpick between his lips. "But he's probably into a lot of girls. His phone beeps more often than R2D2."

Charlie wondered if there had been any scientific advances in recent years on love potions that actually worked. She'd ask her fellow IM's. Someone had to be making progress with pheromones in a lab somewhere.

Darwin executed a hard left in the PAP, sending Charlie's puff-sleeved shoulder into contact with his blazer-covered one. An electric surge of longing rippled through Charlie's arm and shot through her body, down to her toes. She snuck a peek at Darwin and saw a dimple sinking deeper into his cheek as a lopsided smile emerged on his mouth—a sure sign that he felt it, too.

"Remember when we built that house in the favelas?" He sighed wistfully.

Charlie nodded, her mind traveling back to the slums outside of Rio where shacks made of nothing more than cardboard and corrugated metal dotted the mountains. She and Darwin had spent a week working with other volunteers to construct a house for a family with six kids. They'd hammered nails and drilled screws in hundred-degree heat, and Darwin had even injured himself when a cinder block fell on his foot, but it was all worth it when the family saw the simple house once it was built. The mom and the two oldest kids burst into tears, hugging Charlie, Darwin, and the rest of the crew over and over.

"Of course I remember. That was amazing," Charlie said quietly. "I hope we can do something like that again this summer."

"I was just thinking about the foundation of that house. How we had to flatten it and measure it a thousand times before pouring the concrete. And then, the rest was easy."

"Yeah. . . ," Charlie murmured, not quite sure where Darwin was going. It hadn't been that easy to build the rest of the house. And more experienced people did a lot of the hard stuff, but she guessed she saw his point. In some ways,

Charlie thought, they were so different. He could be so enigmatic and abstract, where she was all about practicality. He was drawn to music and philosophy, and she liked taking stuff apart and rebuilding it, working with her hands to get tangible results.

"That's what I want. With you. I want us to build our foundation again, to make it rock solid." His hazel eyes met hers, and Charlie was surprised to see they shone with emotion. "Once our foundation is strong, we can do anything. We can build our dreams."

Charlie swallowed hard, pushing a pining ache for him back down her throat. "I want that, too."

Darwin leaned toward her, his knee touching hers. She shifted it away, pretending not to notice what was happening. His eyes searched hers out, but she looked down at the clear floor of the PAP, her eyes focusing on a group of three Alpha girls chasing Dingo on the beach.

"Charlie?"

"What?" She looked up, plastering a look of innocence across her features.

"Then why are you being so distant?!" Darwin furrowed his brow.

"I thought you understood. I thought we had an agreement." Her voice was flat and emotionless, but inside her heart was whirling faster than a weathervane during a lightning storm. Why couldn't Darwin wait a tiny bit longer?

He rolled his eyes and made a sound in the back of his throat that sounded like he was choking on exasperation. "What agreement?"

"We decided we would play it cool until Allie was over you, remember?"

Darwin shook his head. On the Darwin-ometer, Charlie knew that after anger came stony, furious silence.

"I don't want to be accused of stealing my best friend's crush!"

"But didn't Allie steal *your* crush?"

"No," Charlie said quietly, trying to calm things down before Darwin's iron curtain fully descended. "I set her up with you when we were broken up, remember? I encouraged it. . . ." Charlie sighed, grasping for the right words. It sounded crazy in retrospect, but at the time it seemed to make sense to set up Allie and Darwin. Connecting him with Allie had been Charlie's only way to keep him close, to make him happy after she'd dumped him.

"And now, she's more important to you than I am." Darwin's voice had less warmth than the dry ice they kept in the lab.

"You know that's not—" Suddenly the plane dipped sharply, interrupting Charlie's retort. "What's happening?" she whispered. She gripped Darwin's arm, hard. What if they crashed? After all her sneaking around, it would be all over school in seconds! Pictures of their mangled bodies would be e-mailed to every aPod on the island, and then leaked to the tabloids. At least in that scenario, Charlie wouldn't have to deal with the fallout from Allie. Dead people were forgiven all betrayals, right?

"I'm landing," Darwin said coldly, straightening the plane out and cruising west. Before Charlie could think of what to say to make things right again, to rally Darwin's spirits and make him believe that they would be together just as soon as Allie was over her fixation, the bubble-shaped plane touched down on the octagonal landing pad on the far side of the island. Charlie looked out the window at the Pavilion in the distance, its lighted exterior like a lighthouse. The landing pad here was deep in the jungle, on the wild side of the island, away from prying eyes but also uncomfortably far from campus.

"Darwin, I—"

"Just don't, Charlie. I need some time to think. *Alone*." And before Charlie could utter another word, Darwin popped open the door hatch. She gripped the white foam armrests as the round PAP made contact with the ground.

Charlie blinked, taking in their surroundings. There was nothing but jungle surrounding them. Howler monkeys leapt happily from tree to tree. For a moment she imagined herself and Darwin living among them, foraging for berries and sleeping under the stars. She snapped out of her wishful reverie when Darwin's tanned arm reached over her flight suit, opening the passenger door. This time, Darwin was careful not to touch any part of her. He practically pushed her out of the plane with the hate rays shooting out of his eyes.

"Fine. I'll walk home," Charlie said, biting the inside of her cheek. Dropping her in the middle of the jungle wasn't Darwin: It was like an impostor had taken over his body. She shook her head, wondering what else the new Darwin was capable of. She walked a few paces away from the plane, then turned around and shot Darwin one last look. She half-expected him to change his mind, to hop out, too. Soon, she thought, they would have round two (or was it ten?) of the Allie vs. Darwin argument. But Darwin's face was as impenetrable as a high-security firewall. He blinked, flashed her a hard look, and started the PAP up again, pulling the door shut.

Her mouth twisted into a scribble of disbelief, Charlie watched as the PAP rose higher and higher into the air until it was so tiny it might as well have been a helium balloon.

How could Darwin abandon her in the middle of the jungle? Charlie shook her brown waves uncomprehendingly and started the long walk back to Jackie O. She squinted at the sun, already low in the sky. She might make it home before nightfall, if she hustled. But as she set one clear gladiator sandal in front of the other, something caught her eye: Darwin had set up a whole tent for them. There was a

Bunsen burner, a sandwich press, some bread, and a jar of Nutella. He was going to make their favorite snack out here in the jungle.

Charlie wanted to scream, to laugh, and to cry, all at the same time. Darwin thought they could pick up their relationship right where it had left off by ignoring everything that happened between them. But something had changed. Maybe Charlie had changed. Maybe she'd become an Alpha after all. Like her life these days, her allegiances weren't as clear-cut as they used to be. Maybe she and Darwin *weren't* soul mates. Maybe Charlie's plan for them to be together seemed ridiculous because they weren't meant to be.

Charlie stared through a veil of tears at the vines running on either side of the narrow jungle path. The jungle had seemed so inviting when she floated above it with Darwin, but now the greenery threatened to swallow her up. Overhead, Darwin's PAP floated through the hazy orange light of sunset like a fragile soap bubble destined to pop.

Her hope floating away with Darwin's plane, Charlie fastened her eyes back on the dimly lit jungle path ahead of her. Flying solo was scary, but for the first time she knew how to navigate Alpha Academy on her own.

14

Still smiling after Syd's fart-fleeing exit, Skye finished her cool-down routine and began to pack up for another long soak in the spa. She shoved her toe shoes and hoodie into her metallic red tote and slid a pair of shimmery gray yoga pants on over her dance shorts.

"Let's bounce," Tweety suggested, yanking her long black hair out of its tight bun and high-kicking in the direction of the elevator. "I scream for steam."

"Be right there," Skye murmured. She glanced at Mimi making notes on a touch-screen tablet before she bent down to strap on her clear gladiator sandals. After her cringe-inducing blunder during the final routine, Skye wanted to keep a low profile and get as far away from Mimi as possible.

Sandals secured, Skye shot a look at Triple in her gold dance skirt and plunging gold leo. She was still in cool-down mode, doggedly folding her body over one outstretched leg and then the other. Triple treated her stretching routine with the same militaristic fervor she had for dance practice. "Try not to stink up the joint," Triple muttered as Skye glided past.

Skye shot her eyes toward the ceiling and groped for a quick comeback. "The only way it would stink is if *you* joined us." She kept her voice low so Mimi wouldn't hear. She quickened her pace and cut a path to the elevator, her aquamarine eyes sliding away from the dancing diva like water on a windshield.

Walking fast, Skye almost ran headlong into Mimi, who wielded her tablet like a shield. "Skye, can you stay a moment? You too, Andrea."

"I wish I could—" Skye started, but her voice dissolved faster than Splenda in the face of Mimi's disapproving frown.

Skye shot a pained look at Tweety and Ophie, who stood waiting by the elevator with their brows knitted in sympathy. "I'll meet you in the steam room," she called, and suddenly she was alone in the studio with Mimi and Mini-Mimi. Her heart thundered in her ears as she tried to remain calm.

Mimi cleared her throat and tapped on her tablet with two ringed fingers. "I thought you were finally making progress, but it's not enough."

Of course, I've been distracted, Skye wanted to yell. *I've been dragging a wet blanket around all week!* But she just nodded and looked at the clear floor and the palm fronds scraping the underside of the glass studio from below.

"I'm going to give you one more chance," Mimi continued, her bangled wrists jingling ominously. "You need to prove to me that you belong at Alpha Academy. That what I saw in your application video is something you can recapture."

"Um, Mimi?" Triple piped up, her almond-shaped eyes aimed at the EXIT sign even as her mouth formed a butt-kissy smile. "Do I need to be here? I was hoping to get to the Pilates Reformer at the gym before—"

"I'm getting to that," Mimi said, putting one graceful hand on Skye's shoulder and one on Triple's. Skye wished Mimi would just get on with it. "For the next week, Andrea," Mimi continued, smiling proudly like she'd just come up with a road map for world peace, "Skye belongs to you."

"What?!" both girls said at once.

"She will follow your dance regimen to the letter. NO social activities. One hundred percent focus. If she doesn't improve," Mimi paused for dramatic effect, pursing her lip-sticked mouth, "you will *both* be kicked out."

"What?!" they said again. For once, Skye and Triple were in complete agreement. This was crazy!

"Why should I be responsible for *her?*" Triple whined, her eyes filling with frustrated tears. "That's insane!"

"What about the Muse Cruise?" Skye yelled, her voice

strangled and panicked. It was next weekend, and the whole school would be there! How could Mimi deprive them of a reward like that?

"Definitely not in your future, Skye. This is about showing restraint and discipline. And Andrea, we are not soloists. We are a *troupe*. When one person falters, we all falter. I think you'll both grow from this challenge."

Grow!? You mean grow to hate you, each other, and our lives? Skye clasped her hands together to keep them from shaking with fury. She was so humiliated, insulted, and horrified by Mimi's plan that she couldn't speak. A wad of anger had plugged up her throat like a cotton ball on a bottle of polish remover.

Triple spun around, hiding her freely falling tears from the woman who had caused them. "But Mimi—" she said quietly, already defeated.

Mimi headed toward her office, a small room off the main cube. She paused in the doorway and added one more nail in the coffin. "This isn't up for discussion, ladies. Do it, or leave the Academy."

The two dancers grabbed their things and stepped silently into the elevator. As the doors began to close, Skye's eyes darted wildly around the room she'd once considered a haven. Now, it just looked like a cage.

"I cannot believe this!" Triple wailed as they made their way to ground level.

"How do you think *I* feel? It's like she's put me into special ed!" Skye hissed hatefully. Her throat and chest were hot with shame. "Let's just pretend to go along with it while we practice on our own," she said. The only way to get through the next week was to hope Mimi would forget about it.

"No way," Triple said firmly, her voice hard as tempered steel. "This is *not* special ed. This is boot camp."

The doors whooshed open and they stepped out into the hot afternoon, the smell of jasmine and wild grapefruit crowding their senses. Skye felt beaten. Trapped. And she didn't have any fight left in her. There was nothing she could do now but accept Mimi's challenge.

She shut her tear-filled eyes for a moment, wishing Triple would disappear into thin air. But when she opened them again, the sight of Triple standing there was exponentially worse. Behind Triple, Syd's Vans kicked up dust as he ran toward her clutching a paper bag.

"Hello, my darling," Syd panted, looking deliriously proud of himself. "I'm so glad I caught you! I thought you might need this."

Unless Syd had brought her a magic lamp with three wishes inside, Skye wasn't interested. She opened the bag and pulled out a box of Gas-X.

"It wasn't easy to find this on the island. But lucky for you, I have connections. It should help with your, uh, *problem*." Syd blushed deeply, grinning shyly at Skye.

Ugh! Syd was like the postal service: Not rain, nor sleet, nor deadly farts could keep him from delivering his sickly adoration. "Thanks, Sydney."

"I don't think so." Triple swooped in like a romantic wrecking ball, wedging her tall frame between Skye and Syd. She grabbed the box and crushed it in her angry fist. "The only thing that's going to help Skye now is *me*. Syd, consider yourself back on the market."

Triple grabbed Skye's arm and started pulling her down the path toward the gym. "Time for Pilates," she grunted, and while the last thing Skye wanted was to be stuck in the gym with Sergeant Triple, she sensed an opportunity.

"Nooo!" Skye moaned theatrically, stretching her other arm back toward Syd and channeling her inner Bella Swan. "I need him, Triple!"

"Too bad!" Triple winked, a mischievous smile playing on her lips. "Remember what Mimi said? If you don't do what I say, we'll both get expelled. And then you'll never see Syd again!"

Syd's eyes filled with tears as he waved at Skye. "I'll wait for you forever!"

"Don't bother," Triple yelled, rushing farther and farther down the path with Skye in tow.

Syd began to back away, his face pained and heart-broken.

Skye called after him one last time. "Just remember, Triple broke your heart, not me!"

Syd nodded, overcome with emotion. He turned to sob-run in the opposite direction.

Yes! Yes! Yes! Skye may have to be chained to Triple for the rest of the week, but at least her Syd-shackles had been cut. "Triple, that was ah-mazing! He's really gone!"

Triple elbowed Skye's arms away and glared at her, already back in drill-sergeant mode. "Being done with boys doesn't mean you can hit on *me*!"

"I'm just trying to thank you." Skye backed off and studied Triple's high cheekbones and determined eyes, wondering if maybe she'd misjudged her roommate's self-absorption. "How did you know I wanted to ditch Syd, anyway?"

"I'm not an idiot," muttered Triple, rolling her eyes and spinning around to lead the way down the path to the gym. "I have ears. Besides, he was going to get in the way of our workout regimen. Now march—we're five minutes behind schedule."

Skye nodded, already annoyed by Triple again. Was it that the girl didn't know how to make friends, or that she just didn't want any? Triple was harder to read than a first-generation Kindle.

As Skye trudged behind Triple toward the gym, staring at her perfect dancer's calves, she sigh-fretted in anticipation of what was sure to be an excruciating week. Now that she'd said sayonara to Syd, she needed to figure out how to get out from under Triple's perfectly manicured thumb. As she scurried to keep up with her new taskmaster, Skye began to brainstorm ways to give boot camp the boot.

HAD No. 12: Ditch Triple. On the double.

15

NORTH SHORE JUNGLE
CREATIVE WRITING FUSELAGE
TUESDAY, OCTOBER 5TH
10:07 A.M.

For once, Allie was early to class. She'd hurried through the sun-speckled jungle whispering the lines of a monologue Careen assigned her, and stopped short at the base of the enormous banyan tree that held the fuselage of a Boeing 747 high in its branches. The side of the repurposed aircraft read *Brazille Industries: Empowering Women to Aim High* in sparkling gold script. Through the glass, Allie spotted the über-serious Hannah Hesse, a published poet and budding novelist who treated writing workshops like they were oxygen—essential to life on this planet. Unfortunately for Allie, slouched in an airline seat across from Hannah was AJ, still wearing her dingy crocheted tam pulled low over her scraggly black waves.

Allie sniffed the air, but she couldn't detect Darwin's cinnamon scent lurking under the smells of rotting passion fruit, mud, and peeling tree bark. After applying a quick coat of lip gloss and a hefty dose of jungle-germ-killing Purell, Allie climbed the spiral staircase carved into the trunk of the tree. The holographic walls of the fuselage had been programmed to project images of delicate cherry blossom petals swirling in the wind.

"Hey Hannah," Allie said, pointedly ignoring AJ as she slid her narrow hips into one of the eight airplane seats in the center of the room.

Hannah lay collapsed on her back on a forest green couch along one wall of the fuselage. All around her were scattered sheets of paper covered with double-spaced prose. Her pierced nose crinkled in agitation as she nibbled the ink-black nails of one hand and wielded a red pen in the other. "I've been here all night," Hannah said in her scratchy voice, her gray eyes pink and raw around the rims. "I skipped my first two periods to try to finish my naw-vel, but I just can't seem to . . ." She trailed off and stared at the ceiling, her voice sounding raspier than ever, as if her windpipe had been crushed along with her plotlines.

"Allie's not really a writer," interrupted AJ in her high-pitched baby voice, "but maybe I can help. I have a lot of experience with writer's block."

As Hannah unspooled the details of her latest writing crisis, Allie rolled her eyes and wished a large, heavy writer's block would fall on AJ's head. She pulled her electronic writing tablet out of the tray table compartment of her airline seat and started a hate-doodle of a tiny girl being attacked by a giant crocheted hat. But AJ was right about one thing: Allie *wasn't* a writer. Now that she had fully committed to the dramatic arts, she had less patience for this class than ever. As an actress, writing was her food—not her craft. Writers gave actors something to chew on, and Allie had always liked to be waited on.

A few other writing students trickled in behind Keifer, whose novel *Fifth Avenue Happenstance* had been translated into eighteen languages by the time she was twenty-three. Keifer stood at the front of the room, her slim, angular body and asymmetrical bob partially obscuring the oversized LCD chalkboard behind her.

"Get your tablets out, geniuses. It's time to let our souls sing." Keifer pushed her choppy black bangs away from her face. Allie wondered if the woman cut her own hair, and if she used gardening shears, but just then Charlie walked into the room and slid into the seat next to hers. Seconds later, Darwin showed up and snagged the last seat across the circle.

"Sorry I'm late." He shrug-grimaced at Keifer as he took a toothpick out of his mouth and put it into the pocket of his navy blue blazer. Allie stared at Darwin, turning her lips up slightly and angling her head one quarter to the right. Careen had told her that was the perfect position for paparazzi pictures and head shots, but Darwin's eyes bounced from Keifer to his writing tablet to the floor. Had her fake love toward Mel already made him insecure around her? Allie kicked Charlie's foot, wanting to thank her again for crafting such a brilliant plan.

"You're right on time, Darwin." Keifer reassured him. "We were just getting started." She stepped to one side of the LCD board and placed a silver electronic thimble on her index finger. "Or should I say, *write on time?*" She turned around and quickly wrote those very words in glowing script on the LCD screen.

Allie fished her own writing thimble out of the little compartment of her writing tablet and stuck it on her finger, praying that today's assignment would be painless.

"Today, we're going to learn how we can say so much by saying very little."

Huh? Allie glared at AJ across from her, who was nodding furiously and writing down everything Keifer said on her tablet. She could smell the green goblin's aroma of lavender oil and unwashed hair all the way across the room.

Keifer continued. "We're going to write a haiku. Take inspiration from the cherry blossom petals falling all around you." Keifer turned a knob on the hologram panel and suddenly the whole room was filled with swirling white and pink petals. The class oohed and aahed. Allie tried again to get Darwin's attention, but he stared down at his tablet, obviously deep in thought. Or, Allie hoped, drowning in a pool of jealousy.

Keifer pursed her cupid's bow–shaped lips and raised a sculpted eyebrow. "You're familiar with haiku, right? It's a Japanese poetic form composed of a line with five syllables, a line with seven syllables, and then another line with five. Your assignment right now is to write a haiku about yellow."

Predictably, Hannah's goth-tipped hand shot into the air. "Can you be more specific, Keifer? How yellow makes us feel? Or, like, things that are yellow? Or what colors make up yellow?"

"All of that is up to you. Don't overthink it. *Feel* it! Annnd . . ." Keifer pressed the digital timer icon on the LCD board and it began to count down from four minutes. "Write!"

Allie raised her thimble-covered finger in the air, a tide of ideas rising dangerously fast in her mind. So many feelings were competing in her brain, it was hard to pick just one. She thought of how much she'd rather be onstage right now. How much she wanted Darwin to look up from his tablet and smile at her. How she wished she knew why Charlie was so preoccupied that she couldn't take a moment to acknowledge her. How she wished AJ would take off her icky hat and begin a love affair with Ivory soap.

Beep!

Ugh! The timer ran out, sending Allie's ideas swirling, and sucking the whole confused mess down the drain like gray bathwater.

Allie blinked down at her tablet—empty except for her half-finished doodle of AJ. She had nothing.

She scooted down in her chair and made her eyes focus anywhere but Keifer, hoping she would call on someone else.

"Charlie, why don't you start?"

Whew.

Charlie fidgeted in her seat, twirling a brown wave between two fingers. "Okay:

Yellow is my heart

Afraid of losing your love

Still, I set you free."

Keifer let silence fill the breezy fuselage for a moment before responding. "Nice. I like that you interpreted the color as the emotion of cowardice. Very creative."

Charlie blushed and nodded, her eyes still trained on the floor. She was so modest!

Allie's gaze crept back to Darwin, who was tapping his thimble on his desk. His eyes were hooded and stormy.

Allie crossed and uncrossed her legs under her tray table, wondering if she'd gone too far with her Mel-flirtation. She cleared her throat, hoping to get Darwin to look at her so she could reassure him that he still had a chance. It worked—

Darwin finally looked up, his eyes making contact with Allie's as she flashed him her sweetest, most benevolent smile. The one she reserved for back-to-school JCPenney ads and holiday photos. But it was as if she was cellophane. Darwin looked straight through her.

"AJ, let's hear what you conjured up under that hat of yours."

Why did everyone on earth feel the need to kiss AJ's flat little butt? Allie put her thimble to her mouth and bit it, hoping AJ had written something lame.

"Her hair is yellow
Typical of a mall girl
She's always posing."

AJ looked up from her tablet and glared at Allie, as if it wasn't already obvious that the haiku was about her. Allie's heart began beating out S.O.S. and she felt her face turning red with anger and shame. *Doesn't AJ have other people to make miserable?*

"Huh," Keifer said, cocking her head at AJ and narrowing her pale blue eyes. "Interesting. A departure from your usual themes of environmentalism and love. What was your inspiration?"

"Well," AJ drawled, burrowing one finger under her giant hat and scratching her head, "I'm still working through the personal violation of having my identity stolen. I'm trying to recover through my *art*."

Oh please! Allie sneer-snorted as her eyes shot sky-ward. A few girls in class, including Hannah, nodded like they knew what AJ was talking about firsthand. Allie felt an angry blush crawl up her neck and spread through her cheeks. This was too much!

Allie was like a geyser. She could only stand so much pressure before she blew up. But this time she felt confidence brewing inside her. Her voice calm and clear, she spat back a retort. "Get over it! I was acting, okay? Move on already!"

AJ rolled her moss-green eyes and opened her tiny mouth to respond, but Keifer beat her to the punch. "Two more syllables and that would have been a perfect haiku," she mused.

Really? Allie managed a tight smile for Keifer.

"Your words have power, Allie. Work on it."

Allie took her thimble off. Even though it was embarrassing to have to defend herself against AJ, at least it had gotten her out of writing a haiku!

Keifer moved on. "Darwin, we haven't heard from you in a while."

Darwin sighed. "Okay."

"Yellow Lab you're mine.

I rescued you from the road.

Saving makes me love."

"Tell us where that comes from," said Keifer, looking

out the glassless window of the fuselage as the sounds of screeching macaws drifted in.

"A couple of years ago, I rescued a yellow Lab that was hit by a car. I pledged my undying loyalty to it. I wanted it to know I would take care of it for the rest of its life."

The freckle above his lip bounced as he relived the emotion of saving the dog. His hazel eyes radiated goodness—he was a somber superhero, with magical healing hands that saved the lives of animals. He'd be able to heal Allie from the trauma she'd suffered with Fletcher and during her identity-theft period at Alpha Academy. As soon as she figured out how to get back together with him, they would heal each other.

"Unfortunately, the dog's owner came and took him home. But something about rescuing this old dog made me attached, in a major way. It was like we were destined to find one another. He needed someone, and I happened to be there."

That was *it*! Allie's heart bloomed in her chest like a daffodil shooting out of the ground after a long, cold winter. All Allie needed to do was pretend to be as injured as Old Yeller. If she needed rescuing, Darwin would automatically respond—it was in his DNA to take care of people. And after he rescued her, he would think they were destined to be together. She sat back in her airplane seat and grinned, spinning her blond hair into a high knot on top of her head. She couldn't wait to tell Charlie about the new plan.

Allie opened up the compartment on her tablet and pulled out her thimble again. Now that she had a reason to write, the words flowed quickly.

Be the wounded doggie and lure the rescuing hero!

"To be continued!" Keifer announced, breaking Allie's concentration. "Class dismissed. Work on these tonight, and tomorrow we'll turn them into sonnets!"

"Ready?" Charlie stood in front of Allie's chair, an eager smile on her face. She hopped from one foot to the other, looking more than ready to bail.

"Yeah." Allie stood up and leaned in close to Charlie so none of the other writers would overhear. "I figured out a plan for—"

"Let's get a move on," Charlie cut her off. Her brown eyes darted around distractedly. "I mean, tell me in a minute. I want to get out of this airplane and back to earth."

"Okay. . . ." Allie wondered why Charlie was so impatient. Out of the corner of her eye she saw Darwin hustling down the spiral staircase and hurrying away.

When Charlie and Allie reached the bottom of the tree, Allie was surprised to see Mel leaning against the gnarled trunk, checking his aPod. He wore his Alphas blazer over a lemon-yellow button-down, khaki shorts, and flip-flops, and his white-blond hair almost glowed in the dappled, leaf-speckled shade of the tree. Not that Allie cared. She was too busy working out the details of her pooch ploy to worry about faux-flirting her way into Mel's heart.

"Hey Mel," Charlie said, doing a terrible job of feigning surprise. "Are you here to see Darwin?"

"Not exactly," Mel said, his chiseled cheeks lifting in a smile as he aimed his lavender eyes straight at Allie.

Allie smiled back at him, but her legs itched to catch up with Darwin. She stuck her hands in the pockets of her pleated mini and cleared her throat. Her eyes shot from Charlie to Mel and back again. Both of them looked at her expectantly.

"Well, nice seeing you," she finally said, giving Mel a tight smile. "Gotta run!"

"Maybe Mel should walk you to acting class," Charlie suggested a little too eagerly.

"Sure, I could do that," Mel said, nodding. "It's kind of on my way."

"Nah." Allie shook her head. "I have a monologue to memorize. Gotta do it solo, of course! Bye!"

Without waiting for a reply, Allie whirled around on the toe of her gladiator sandal and took off, power-walking down the path and not looking back. Charlie was wrong—faking an interest in Mel wasn't where Allie's acting talents were needed. She took a breath of the heavy jungle air and moved her focus back to Operation Puppy Love.

Inspiration! Or was it motivation? Allie couldn't remember what actors said. She smiled to herself as she walked, realizing that it didn't matter—she had them both.

16

"Music—on!" In the middle of Lake Alpha, surrounded by tree-capped mountains and with nothing over her head except Mimi's threats of expulsion, a clear blue sky, and a sparkly black swim cap to protect her blow-out, Triple straddled her surfboard like it was a horse and she was a corseted woman in the eighteenth century. She directed her command to the round waterproof aPod amplifier floating like a buoy a few feet away, where "I Will Survive" blasted from the speakers.

Skye crouched into position, her back arched and her arms pressed tightly together, and snuck a look at Triple before tucking her head down between her shoulder blades.

Apparently, Triple owned the water just like she owned the dance studio. Triple's black wetsuit was totally dry from the waist up—she hadn't gotten so much as a droplet of water on it after swimming out to the middle of Lake Alpha with Skye an hour ago. Skye's skimpy gold string bikini wasn't so lucky. Shivering and rubbing her hands along her upper arms to try to generate some heat, Skye looked longingly toward the narrow strip of white sand on the shore, where a pile of towels, hoodies, and yoga pants awaited them.

"Tell me why we keep doing the routine to Gaynor and not Gaga?" Skye whined, clawing at the air as a tiny gust of wind threatened to topple her off the shiny white surfboard.

One of Triple's tawny, slender arms twitched in time with the music, while the other remained firmly planted on her perfectly proportioned hip. She narrowed her golden eyes and shot Skye a look that said *more dance, less talk.*

"Because," Triple growled, "relying on the music to dictate your dancing is one of many bad habits we're trying to break. Now stop stalling! Keep your focus!"

Skye sighed, squinting her teal eyes at the pine-topped mountains ringing the lake and watching the air-chairs crawl up Mount Olympus like ants on an anthill. She closed her eyes and tried to astrally project herself into one of the chairs, but when she opened them she hadn't moved an inch from the gently rocking surfboard.

Taking a deep breath of pine-scented air, Skye tensed her muscles and concentrated on keeping her balance on the swaying board. The surfboard routine was all about balance. When she practiced the routine in the llama cage, surrounded by well-placed llama poop, it was all about accuracy. One wrong step, and shoes became ews. When she did the routine in the sauna wearing ankle weights, it was all about endurance.

And when she did the routine in her sleep, it was all about insanity.

For the past twenty-four hours, Triple had been following Skye around, tapping notes into her aPod and creating a spreadsheet that she may as well have called *Reasons Skye Sucks and Should Give Up Dancing for a Career as a Dental Hygienist.*

Skye had no idea how she was supposed to get through five more days of one-on-one rehearsals with Triple. Unlike Gloria, Skye wouldn't survive.

"And a-one, two, three, and four!" yelled Triple, raising a pair of huge waterproof binoculars to her eyes so she could view Skye's moves in sharp detail. "Remember, strong core! Fluid arms!"

Skye nodded. When this week was over, she'd either be good enough for Alvin Ailey or nuts enough for Alvin and the Chipmunks.

As Gloria began to belt, Skye started the routine. Her feet were like suction cups on the surfboard, stepping and sliding so quickly and carefully that the surfboard stayed horizontal, miraculously not tipping her into the deep.

At first I was afraid, I was petrified
Kept thinking I could never live without you by my side

Determination to stay afloat coursing through her chilled veins, Skye hip-swiveled, executed a perfect three-sixty-degree turn, and did a rocker-chic faux-headbanger dip-one-two, her arms pounding the air above her bunned hair. And then she felt it. The board began to go vertical, sliding out from under her like a tablecloth yanked out from a set table by a magician.

"*Nooo!*" Skye scream-moaned loud enough to shake the pine trees on top of Mount Olympus. She clawed desperately at the board with her toes, trying to find her center, but it plunged nose-first into the water. And a millisecond later, so did Skye.

Sputtering and choking as she surfaced, Skye swam-spun around until she spotted Triple, then grabbed the board and swam over to Her Highness. Her Dryness was more like it.

"Nice recovery," Triple smirk-smiled. "We've made progress, even if it doesn't seem like it. You stayed on a lot longer than the first five times."

"Have you always been this sadistic, or do I bring it out in you?" Skye swam her board closer to Triple's and was about to "accidentally" kick a mouthful of water at the dance diva, when Triple pointed a pale orange coral reef–colored fingernail across the lake.

"Check it," Triple whisper-smiled, pulling her binoculars off and handing them to Skye, pointing over Skye's right shoulders. "Turn around. Don't say I never gave you anything."

"You gave me sore quads, paranoia that Mimi hates me, and now a good chance of getting pneumonia. . . ." Skye could have extended her list for days, but when she dog-paddled her board to face east, she fell silent. The *Joan of Arc*, Shira's yacht, was slicing a smooth path through the lake. She squinted, and through the fringe of her waterproof-mascara-coated lashes, she could make out two figures sprawled out on anchor-shaped couches on the yacht's deck. "Who is it?"

"Binoculars, Einstein," eye-rolled Triple.

"Ohmuhgud." Holy toe shoes, Syd was with another girl! Skye's heart did a joyous tour glissade. Syd and Seraphina Hernandez-Rosenblatt—a successful fashion designer and budding neuroscientist determined to bridge the gap between brain chemistry and ready-to-wear—looked cozier than a Snuggie commercial. They were passing *The Notebook* back and forth and looked like they were reading aloud. To each other. Skye focused the binoculars to sharpen her view and make sure her eyes weren't playing tricks on her. She smiled as she saw a lone tear drip down Syd's chiseled cheek, while Seraphina had already squeezed out several that were now streaking her Botticelli-beautiful face.

"Looks like Syd moved on after all," Triple remarked, paddling closer to Skye.

"I cannot believe it," Skye muttered. Sure, she was thrilled to be rid of Syd, but what about all those poems he wrote, all his talk of *undying love* for Skye? "I guess he wasn't that into me after all."

"No, he was definitely into you. Those emo boys give it all away up front. They're obsessed with being in love, more than anything else. They really just need a girl around to stroke their fragile egos."

"I *so* am not the girl for that job," said Skye, smiling.

"Nope." Triple shook her head. "You have major goals."

"He didn't even wait a day!" Skye giggled, delirious with the realization that her Syd saga was over.

Triple's eyes crinkled up in the corners with mirth and when they met Skye's, the two girls began to giggle uncontrollably. Their laughter soon escalated to hysterical guffaws, which quickly turned to the kind of shaking, silent laughter you only did with real friends. Skye paddled over to Triple and gave her a celebratory hug that nearly sent both of them tipping into the lake. Finally, she was free of Suffocating Syd, and Triple was the one who'd made it happen. The girl had drive, and drive meant power.

When the *Joan* passed them, Skye looked at her frenemy: With her perfect tawny complexion, her fab and always-flawless blow-out, her long limbs that could dance any routine perfectly after seeing it just once, and her wide yet rare smile capped off with twinkling golden eyes,

Triple was a stunner. When Triple let loose and laughed, her beauty—both inner and outer—radiated over the lake like an enchanted mist.

"One more peek," Skye said. "Just to see if they're kissing yet." She put the binoculars to her eyes once more, but this time what she saw wiped the smile off her face like her dance towel removed perspiration after a long workout. Skye scowled, her peaceful moment long gone, replaced by a sinking feeling, along with the hope that the *Joan* might sink along with her heart. Syd and Seraphina weren't alone on the yacht. Taz was there, too. With company.

Through the round lenses, three others appeared on deck just a few feet away from Syd and sobbing Seraphina. Skye frowned, focusing the binoculars on Taz's chiseled jaw, surrounded on both sides by the white-blond Trapezoid twins. The Trapezoids (a stage name, of course) were slender, willowy girls who had been raised in a traveling circus family. They were trapeze artists and could swallow fire, and after achieving worldwide YouTube celebrity at age thirteen, they'd gone on to raise millions of dollars for Katrina victims by becoming world-class concert promoters. They brought new meaning to a bunch of words that Skye knew also applied to her: *blonde, party person, boy magnet.* And now they were draped all over Taz like a pair of tacky curtains.

"Forget Taz. Let's run through it one more time. . . ."

Triple fiddled with the buttons on the aPod, but Skye didn't have the strength to get back up on her board. She shivered, suddenly desperate to get out of the lake, which had gone from a tepid bath to a refrigerated Brita in a matter of seconds.

"Can we call it a day?" she tried, wiggling her eyebrows as she attempted to put the image of Taz and the twins on simmer instead of a rolling boil.

"Nawt a chance!" Triple's smile was long gone now, along with any friendship that might have begun to blossom between them.

Skye shivered again, blinking back tears and watching with unsurprised eyes as a few dark clouds came rolling in, blocking out what had been—for a moment, anyway—a gloriously blue sky, full of possibility. The only thing that could warm her up now was the thought that soon her week with Triple would be over.

17

"Good morning, creators!" Dr. Irina Gorbachevsky, brilliant nanotechnologist and jolly Alpha Invention Mentor, shouted down from the top of the lab's iridescent spiral staircase. Designed to mimic the shape of a strand of DNA, the staircase spun dramatically up through the center of the enormous lightbulb-shaped room. Like the building itself, the stairs were made entirely from recycled glass, and covered with holographic scientific formulas.

Dr. G pushed her bright green rectangular glasses up the bridge of her nose and smiled, locking her raisin-colored eyes with Charlie's and flashing her favorite student a comforting smile. Dr. G was a pioneer in nanotechnology and string theory, and Charlie smiled back at her warmly. Then she put her hands on her laptop keyboard and readied her fingers to record any words of scientific wisdom Dr. G might have.

"Today," Dr. G continued as she traveled bouncily down the spiral strand of DNA toward her protégées, patting her frizzy gray hair with one of her pudgy hands, "we'll take a

126

break on our own projects and do a brain-stimulating mini-invention session."

The only brain stimulation Charlie had experienced since Darwin dropped her in the jungle was shocks of guilt, confusion, and loneliness. Charlie rolled up the sleeves of her platinum coveralls and spun around on her ergonomic lab stool, her body mimicking her thoughts. She pulled her chocolate brown hair up into a loose ponytail and glanced around the room, waiting for Dr. G to continue.

To the right of Charlie's cubicle was the workstation of Yvette Chan, a spiky-haired cyber-punk obsessed with touch-screen technology, and to her left was Lydia Bjorgstrum, a half-Swedish food scientist who only spoke in monosyllables and worked 24/7 on developing cloning techniques for cuts of meat. The IM's were friendly enough, and Charlie appreciated their passion and their drive, but she couldn't pour her heart out to them. They were more interested in molecules and microscopes than meeting boys.

Charlie sighed and turned back to Dr. G, who had made her way to the invention floor and now stood under the etched-glass section of the lightbulb. It read: *Dream lofty dreams, and as you dream, so shall you become.* Charlie had read and reread the sentence, but right now her only dream was to be able to confide in Allie again. She was so confused—never before had she been less sure about her and Darwin. Too bad the only person she trusted enough to confide in about something this important liked him, too.

For Allie's sake, Charlie wanted to get over Darwin. But no matter how hard she tried, she couldn't figure out how. She looked longingly at the lab's LCD vending machine, where the IM's could type in whatever tool or material they needed, and receive it instantly via delivery from robot lab assistants that looked like white plastic beetles. Charlie wished she could order up a little bit of clarity with a side of emotional glue to repair her breaking heart.

Dr. G yanked her lab coat down along her protuberant tummy and continued with the day's assignment. "I want everyone to invent something small, simple, and stream-lined. Something that will improve your life *today*, instead of changing civilization as we know it. Set your invention intentions first. Remember, sometimes aiming small pro-duces huge results. Look at the Post-it Note!"

The Post-it Note was one of Dr. G's favorite examples of modern-day success. Something as simple as small squares of paper had made billions of dollars, simply because some-one added adhesive. *Simple, elegant, effective*, Dr. G liked to say.

Charlie wrinkled her nose, stood up and headed toward the LCD note board that covered a wall of her workstation. She put a writing thimble on her index finger and began to grope for inspiration.

Improve your life TODAY, she wrote, then ran her palm

over the glowing script and erased the phrase. After a moment, the perfect name for her new invention came to her. It was only thing that could improve her life today, but it would be impossible to invent. Sighing, she wrote it down in big capital letters anyway: *HEARTBREAK HELPER*.

Charlie smiled at the shimmering board for a moment before heading over to her computer to do some research.

She Googled "what makes humans feel happy?" and eagerly read the first fifty hits that seemed to have research on their side. Why hadn't she ever thought to approach her own happiness with the scientific methods she used in her studies?

In a few minutes, Charlie compiled a list of scientifically proven happiness helpers and hastily wrote them in bullet points on her invention board. After she crossed off everything that couldn't be simulated, her list looked like this:

THINGS THAT INCREASE HAPPINESS:
—Smiling (fake smiling leads to real smiling!)
—~~Strong connections to community, friends, and family~~
—~~Sense of purpose~~
—~~Pets, houseplants (though there was that baby seal invented in Japan. . . .)~~
—~~Exercise~~
—~~Nature~~
—Aromatherapy (tangerine!)

Tangerines and smiling. Charlie leaned forward on her lab stool and rested her chin in her palm to think. It wasn't a lot to work with, but it was a start. Charlie opened up the 3–D rendering program on her laptop and began to sketch some ideas. A few minutes of aimless sketching ticked by, but the faces of Darwin and Allie still loomed more 3–D in Charlie's mind than any invention.

Charlie rubbed her tired eyes with fisted hands. She was at a loss. How could she invent something to cure heartbreak when she was such an emotional wreck?

Beep!

A blinking box popped up on her laptop screen. It was Bee, wanting to IM from across the Atlantic in Oxford.

Bee: Hallo luv. How is my brilliant girl?
Charlie: OK . . .
Bee: Just OK?

Charlie didn't want to explain the whole sordid story to her mother. After all, Bee had given up a thirteen-year career as Shira's assistant so that Charlie could attend the Academy. The last thing Charlie wanted was for her mother to think she wasn't serious about her education or that she was compromising her place at the Academy by stewing over Darwin. Besides, her IM window wasn't big enough and her time wasn't unlimited enough to even scratch the surface. So she settled on generic loneliness.

> **Charlie:** Lonely. Miss you. Miss the way things used to be with Darwin.
> **Bee:** In this world, you have to count on yourself for your own happiness. And lucky for you, you inherited your father's talent with his hands.
> **Charlie:** But what if that isn't enough?
> **Bee:** It has to be. You can't depend on anything in life to always go your way, but your talent is yours forever. Make me proud.
> **Charlie:** I will. Promise. Gotta run. Big kiss.

Charlie nibbled on her lower lip and twirled her three cameo bracelets around her wrists—the bracelets were the only things she owned that had belonged to her dad. One bracelet had a picture of Bee from 1980, when her mother looked a lot like Charlie did now. One had a picture of her father in his Royal Navy uniform. And the other cameo was empty. It used to have a picture of Darwin inside it, until Shira forced her to hand it over as a condition of acceptance into the Academy.

Ignoring the crash of a shattered tray of beakers one of the IM's dropped somewhere behind her, Charlie ran her finger along the ivory cameos, desperate for an idea. She looked over her shoulder at her notes on the board. *Smiling . . . tangerine . . . smiling . . . tangerine.*

Suddenly, a lightbulb went off. She had it.

Charlie raced over to the LCD vending machine and punched in the components she needed. A few minutes later, a shiny white lab robot that looked like an ottoman on wheels sped up to her cubicle with all the materials: an oscillating fan, which she would repurpose as an aromatherapy delivery device, and a series of pulleys that Charlie hoped would get a user to smile.

An hour later, Charlie set down her soldering iron and looked up at the clock. She had only a few minutes to test her device. She sat down and put her head through the hole in the helmet she'd rigged up as part of her Heartbreak Helper.

Two tiny plastic prongs pushed Charlie's lips—which had been set in frown mode for so long that they seemed to have lead weights on their corners—into a forced-yet-comfortable smile. Then her own recorded voice said "please close your eyes" and a light mist of tangerine essence filled her nostrils.

Charlie felt ridiculous under her Heartbreak Helper helmet, but after twenty seconds of forced smiling and sniffing tangerines, she had to giggle at the silliness of her synthetic happiness producer. And giggling made her feel . . . happy. Which meant the helmet actually worked! For a few minutes, at least.

When she pulled the Heartbreak Helper off, Charlie did an emotional assessment. She felt a tiny bit less panicked, less miserable, and ever-so-slightly more hopeful that things would be okay, that she would survive this glitch with Darwin and maybe even be a better person for it. Which led her to consider Allie. Post-helmet, Charlie decided that even the Allie question would resolve itself somehow. Allie wouldn't—*couldn't!*—hate Charlie again. Not after everything they'd been through together. Maybe Charlie would manage to make Bee proud after all, even from the middle of the most lopsided love triangle in history.

Charlie stood up and smoothed out her platinum coveralls and a faint smile spread over her lips, no helmet required.

18

Crouched in a deep lunge on the clay track, Allie sniffed the air around her. The smell of the ocean mingled with cut grass in the soft night breeze, almost masking the faint tang of sweaty socks still lingering from the Alphas in Motion class. Allie rose from her lunge and swung her arms around in big circles, fully embracing her performance in the role of Casual Jogger. She had dressed the part, donning a reflective Alphas unitard with matching hood that covered everything but her face in stretchy, shiny silver. Patented by Brazille Industries the unitard pressed down body hair and flab, making the person inside it sleek and fast, all while monitoring body heat, wicking sweat away, and cooling the skin. Her Pro-Woman Sneakers—another Brazille product—beamed an LCD display onto the track just in front of wherever Allie stood, informing her of how many steps she'd taken (46), calories she'd burned (12), and miles she'd completed (.04).

The track was on a low cliff next to the ink-black ocean, and the sounds of crashing waves filled Allie's ears. She cocked her head, hoping to pick up the sound of Darwin's footsteps. She'd heard he came here every day at seven to run. Unable to pick up any Pumas headed her way, Allie began a slow shuffle around the track, hoping she wouldn't break an actual sweat and ruin her eye makeup before Darwin showed up.

But Allie wasn't here to jog. Not for long, anyway. She was here to fall.

Getting into character, she forced her sneakers to pick up the pace, careful to keep her stomach sucked in and her shoulders back as she ran—her unitard didn't leave anything to the imagination. Channeling her inner runner wasn't that hard. All she had to do was *go*. Allie pumped her Lycra-encased arms and forced her legs to bound along the rubberized track. In a few seconds, she was already exhausted.

As the clock ticked, Allie cursed whoever invented such an unpleasant activity. *People do this for fun?* Allie's chest felt like someone had parked a car on it, and her muscles burned so badly she could almost hear them shrieking. Channeling Careen's advice again, Allie tried to turn off her thoughts and pretend that she wasn't about to take a fall on purpose. She needed to look totally natural when she fell in front of Darwin. But what if she broke a tooth? What if she did permanent damage to her face and needed a nose job or a skin graft, and wound up looking like Heidi Montag?

She pressed on and tried to focus on how much Darwin would dig dating a fellow runner—especially one he had *rescued* after a fall. Hopefully, Allie thought as she rounded a bend in the track, he wouldn't notice how red her face was from the exertion, or the unladylike, extra-large beads of sweat pooling on her upper lip and dripping down her chin . . .

Out of nowhere, Allie's thin-soled track shoes skidded on a patch of gravel, and before she knew it, her upper body was sailing out ahead of her while her legs bent back, sending her feet flying into the air behind her. She was falling *for real*, and Darwin wasn't even there to save her! Before she had time to break her fall with her hands, Allie landed chin-first on the clay track.

"Ooof!" She gasped feebly for air. The fall had knocked the wind out of her. She tried to roll over, but found that she didn't have the strength. Allie felt like a giant beetle between two windowpanes—helpless and highly unattractive. She put her arms under her head and moaned into them, wondering where her aPod was and if her injuries were serious enough to warrant a medi-copter to take her off the island. If there was any chance of a chin scar, Allie would demand plastic surgery. Her chin—neither too pointy nor too square—was one of her best features!

With her eyes still closed, Allie realized the ringing in her ears had been replaced by the sound of footsteps. *Darwin!* Not moving a muscle, Allie began to moan louder, suppressing a relieved smile. It wasn't too late to put her rescued-puppy plan back into action.

The footsteps got closer, and moments later two fingers gently pressed against her neck, taking her pulse. Strong hands grabbed her shoulders and turned her around onto her back. Giddy with the romance of the moment, Allie opened her eyes, ready to blurt out a shaken thanks to Darwin for rescuing her. But the boy crouched above her was enshrouded in shadows, his outline backlit by the klieg lights.

Allie blinked hard, suddenly not even sure it was Darwin at all. He was more muscular than usual, and he smelled musky, manly—closer to Dior Homme than cinnamon.

"Thanks," she managed to squeak.

"Are you okay?"

Mel!

"I . . . I think so."

"Let's see if you can sit up."

Allie should have been devastated. Darwin not saving her meant her fall was pointless. Strangely, though, Darwin had all but vanished from her mind.

Mel put his warm hands back on her shoulders and gently helped her up to a seated position. Allie stared into his violet eyes, where she could see her own reflection, suddenly mesmerized by how adorable the boy in front of her was. How competent and mature, and just plain hawt. How could she have dissed him after writing class today? What had she been thinking?

"I'm, um, sorry I ran off earlier today," Allie blurted. "I had a lot on my mind."

"It's cool," Mel murmured. "You're focused on your acting now. That's awesome."

Now Allie might not need to act the part. Looking at Mel, it suddenly seemed as if they were already linked somehow.

Mel cringed as he noticed her knee. "That's pretty deep," he said.

Allie looked down at the bloody wound and shrugged. She couldn't feel any pain whatsoever, just a warm tingle of attraction for her mega-hot savior.

"I wish I had some Purell to clean it out." Mel sighed, patting his pockets. "I left mine at home."

"I have some," said Allie, her heart melting further over their mutual germaphobia. "I never leave home without it."

She dug her Purell bottle out of the tiny pocket in the hip of the running suit, and Mel smiled. Not just with his mouth, but with his eyes.

"Great minds think alike," he said, squirting some on

his hands and then into Allie's cut. "This might sting a little."

"I'm tough," she whispered. And for once, she actually believed it. Mel's square jaw clenched adorably as he concentrated on cleaning her cut knee.

Suddenly remembering her own chin, Allie reached up and patted it with her hand. She brought her fingers in front of her eyes and saw that there was blood there. "Uh-oh," she whispered, her stomach clenching at the thought of facial disfigurement. Why hadn't Mel mentioned the cut on her face? It must be so awful that he didn't want to bring it up.

"You have a tiny scrape on your chin," Mel said as if reading her mind. "It's nothing. Probably be gone by morning. You can still model, don't worry." He smiled at Allie, exposing a row of teeth so white that in the moonlight they almost looked blue.

"Thanks," breathed Allie. "I mean, I don't want to model anymore. But I do hope to act."

"I'm not modeling anymore either," Mel said. "Too boring." Though his abs were swathed in the thick cotton of his workout hoodie, Allie could tell by his posture Mel still sported a six-pack. Maybe even an eight-pack. "My ultimate goal is to open a mall that's better and bigger than the Mall of America." Mel flipped his blond hair out of his eyes and grinned at Allie.

"I've been wishing for a more futuristic mall for years!" Allie squealed, leaning in closer to Mel and getting another whiff of his musky, yummy cologne. "Bigger than the Glendale Galleria, and with more attractions. The time has come."

"Roller coasters, moving sidewalks, a laser light show and planetarium that's woven seamlessly into the shopping experience . . . ," Mel listed, nodding at Allie.

"Exactly! Personal shoppers who do a body and style scan and cross-reference it with every store, robot valet services, salons that allow you to virtually shop while you get highlights . . . sorry, I could go on and on." Allie looked shyly into Mel's eyes, but they weren't bored at all. They were glued on her tighter than the hair extensions she'd gotten for Homecoming last year.

Mel smiled. "It's great to meet someone as passionate about consumerism as I am."

Allie nod-smiled. She wished the two of them could take a PAP to the Santa Ana Shopping Plaza right now and wander through it with some Cold Stone Creamery rocky road ripple (two spoons, one waffle cone), critiquing and improving the mall together.

Mel cleared his throat. "Are you going to the Muse Cruise?"

Allie blush-nodded. *Ohmuhgud.* "Wouldn't miss it."

"Maybe I should go with you." Mel stood up, extended

both of his hands, and pulled Allie up as gently as he'd done earlier. "You know, to help you walk."

Allie nodded, limping closer to Mel as they headed toward campus. And even though Allie was limping, she felt as if she were walking on air.

19

"Music—on!" Triple snapped her manicured fingers and the studio's voice-activated stereo surprised Skye by queuing up "Bad Romance."

This was it. Skye took a shallow breath and rolled her shoulders back, planting her feet on the rubberized studio floor and relishing the fact that cold water and llama poop were nowhere to be found.

A twitchy grin played on Skye's glossed lips. She had this. She knew she did. After a week of dancing nonstop to "I Will Survive," Skye began to dance to the sounds of "Bad Romance" and realized she had absorbed Gloria Gaynor's message—she would survive Mimi's challenge.

Skye stayed ahead of the beat, landing every leap, every turn, each hip-thrust to perfection. She didn't think, she just danced. She didn't groove to the music, the music grooved to her. Every one of her muscles did what she told it to, and as she launched into a tricky quadruple spin during her solo, she knew she owned the routine.

Skye froze in her final position, lying on her side, her back arched, her arms raised in a catlike position. Before Triple said a word, Skye already knew they had done it. Her body told her. Her sculpted arms and abs told her. Her rock-hard glutes applauded. She was in tune with her body to a degree she never had been before. And that, she had to admit, was because of Triple's insane dance boot camp. Skye had been dancing like a maniac all week. She felt lean, tight, and strong. She had never felt more in control of what her body could do. And as Triple's glossed mouth curved into a Crest Whitestrips smile, Skye smiled back. Her whole body applauded, and now Triple clapped, too. Mimi would be blown away.

"Okay," Triple murmured, smile-nodding at Skye. For once, Triple sounded proud, not annoyed.

"Okay . . . what?" Skye prompted, still out of breath from dancing her butt off.

Triple lifted a perfectly plucked brow and shot Skye an amused smile. "Okay, there's nothing wrong with it."

"Come on, Trip. I know it's hard, but can you say something positive for once? After all, this is your accomplishment, too."

Triple blush-smiled, assessing Skye with her almond-shaped golden eyes. "It's perfect. Flawless. Like my hair today." She flipped her blow-out over her right shoulder and stroked it like a security blanket.

"Thank God," Skye said, rolling out of position and onto her back, enjoying the sensation of the cool floor on her sweaty back. "No more boot camp!"

Triple gracefully slid down to the floor, too, elegantly wilting like a calla lily in a vase. "We're done. I don't want you pushing it any more today. We'll just do a light stretching routine every two hours to stay limber and wait for tomorrow to come so you can knock Mimi's tights off."

"Enough!" Skye sat up and almost pounced on her model-perfect drill sergeant. "When have you ever had any fun at this school, Trip?" she demanded, crossing her still-sweaty arms.

"Every day is fun," Triple muttered, folding over her outstretched legs to grab her feet and stretch her calves. "Work is fun. Was it not fun when you stepped in the animal poo? Was it not fun when you nailed the back walkover next to that cactus?"

"Yeah," Skye said dryly, unable to keep her eyes from rolling. "That was ah-mazing." Skye grabbed a towel from her dance bag and dabbed at her face. Work is work, she wanted to shout. *Fun* is fun! "We deserve—no, let me rephrase that—we *need* to have some fun."

"We could paint our nails, I guess," Triple said, holding up a hand for close inspection of her manicure.

"We *could*," Skye said, treading carefully, "or we could go on the Muse Cruise." *There*, she thought. The bomb had been dropped. Now it just had to explode.

Triple shook her head. "Mimi said no."

"Mimi doesn't ever have to *know*," Skye countered, taking care to keep her voice in a non-hysterical register. She had to convince Triple that it was rational, even *sensible*, to go on the cruise. "And she only told us not to because she thought we'd need this time to practice. Well, we practiced until we reached perfection. And science has proven again and again that it's toxic to do too much work with no reward—"

"*Success* is the reward!" Triple shook her head emphatically, her hair swishing along her shoulders like sea grass. As Skye expected, Triple wasn't going to have fun without a fight. It was just how the girl was wired.

Skye narrowed her blue eyes and assessed Triple for the millionth time this week, still unable to figure her out. What was it like to never socialize? To eat and sleep and dance like a robot? Skye had a taste of Triple's militaristic discipline this week, and today, she had a taste of the payoff that came with it. But everyone needed relaxation, didn't they? Skye scanned her frenemy's face, marveling at its perfect symmetry and bone structure, highlighted by Trip's flawless makeup application. Suddenly, she knew how to win her over. She needed to appeal to Triple's vanity. The girl spent

more time on hair and makeup than Lady Gaga herself—
didn't she want a boy to appreciate it for once?

"You look so pretty today," sighed Skye. "You would *own*
that cruise. With the BB's on the market, it's a shame you
won't be there to snag one for yourself." She let her eyes
drift to the window and focused on a pair of finches flirting
in the fronds of an acai palm. Even the birds were flirting!
Wasn't it time for Triple to join them?

"I *do* look good today," Triple conceded quietly. "But I
don't socialize here. I mean, I never have. I wouldn't know
where to start." Her voice quavered and her eyes stuck to
the floor like old chewing gum.

Skye struggled to remain calm, knowing she had begun
to reel the elusive diva-fish on her party line. "You showed
me how you live this week. Now let me teach you a thing
or two."

Skye grabbed Trip's hands and pulled her housemate to
her feet. Triple had helped Skye perfect her dance moves.
Now Skye would repay the favor. She would teach Trip to
loosen up, have fun, and put her high cheekbones and perfect hair to their proper use—shameless flirting!

"Come on," said Skye, smiling with her eyes and aiming
every ounce of her considerable charm at Triple.

Triple sighed and looked sideways at Skye. "I can't
believe I'm going along with this. Fine, let's go. But we can-
not get caught."

Triple had bitten! Skye's heart did a quadruple pirouette, and her body followed suit. Finishing her twirl, Skye landed in second position. "I'm good at a few things. One of them is making a splash at parties. Another one is never getting caught."

Skye grabbed her bag in one hand and Triple's sculpted bicep in the other, hurrying her out of the studio before she changed her mind.

"You'll thank me, I promise," she chirped. For the first time all week, Skye was leading the way. And after Mimi saw her moves, she might even lead the way on the dance floor, too.

20

JACKIE O
POOL
FRIDAY, OCTOBER 8TH
7:17 P.M.

Like a wild salmon trapped in a goldfish bowl, Allie swam fast and furious laps through the chlorinated water of the Jackie O lap pool. Jutting out from the bottom floor of their dome-shaped domicile, the lap pool was surrounded by curved glass walls that revealed a blazing pink sunset offset by swaying black palm fronds. But not even the postcard-pretty sky could make Allie happy tonight.

In an hour, every Alpha and all the BB's would set sail in Shira's faux-cean, enjoying the most inspirational and socially significant event of the semester. Everyone except Allie. She executed a swim-team captain flip when she reached the end of her lap, pushing off the wall of the pool as hard as she could, her arms frustration-flexing out in front of her in an annoyed, aggressive butterfly stroke. She could hardly believe she had resorted to faking sick at a time like this. And all because of her two least favorite letters in the alphabet: A and J.

Allie checked the wall clock—Mel should be here in fifteen minutes with chicken noodle soup and Scattergories, which meant it was time to get out of the pool, go upstairs, and practice her best sick-person sniffle. Ordinarily, the idea of being nursed back from the brink by a gorgeous boy while playing board games would be right up Allie's alley, but not tonight. Tonight, she longed to dance under the moon, to sway on the water and show off her newfound connection with Mel. But she couldn't.

Not after what happened this afternoon.

Allie grabbed the pool's ladder with two hands and quickly hoisted herself out of the pool, automatically activating the motion-activated warming ray that beamed down from the ceiling. Standing under the red glow as the ray's toasty air dried her skin and bathing suit, Allie squeezed her navy blue eyes shut. But the image of AJ rehearsing for the Muse Cruise stayed as vivid as if it were still happening.

Just a couple of hours ago, Allie had walked out of the theater arts mask after rehearsing a monologue with Careen. Still in character and whispering her lines as she walked, she nearly crashed into AJ, who was using the atrium of the mask as a rehearsal space. She was there with Tameeka Sands, her greenest groupie and number-one fan. Rushing past AJ and pretending to leave, Allie had darted behind a fern to listen in. AJ was finishing up singing another new

149

song, and just like the others, it was all about Allie. The last two lines dug into Allie like the claws of a cat, ripping her good mood to shreds.

Here's a role you may want to play, try acting like yourself one day
Kissing you sets boys' lips on fire, nothing burns more than kissing a liar!

Tameeka clapped and whistled. "Nice! I love it," she gushed.

"I've turned my identity theft experience into a song cycle," AJ bragged breathlessly to Tameeka. "I almost have enough for my next album."

So *that* was why AJ was so obsessed with Allie! *Identity Theft* was going to give her another platinum record! Allie fumed, her hands shaking with anger and frustration as she cowered behind the fern.

Tameeka flipped her braids from one shoulder to the other. "We're all victims, if you think about it. We're all trying to steal our identities back from corporate media and stuff."

AJ adjusted her tam, nodding at Tameeka without really hearing her. "Uh-huh. I think this new track will sound great on the cruise."

Say what?!

Allie's heart throbbed, going from dismayed irritation into full-blown panic. If Mel heard AJ's song cycle, he would change his mind about Allie for sure. Somehow, even the silliest sentiments were convincing when set to a strumming guitar. Mel would hum along. He'd wake up the next day singing AJ's lame lyrics. Then he would set Allie aside like she was algebra homework on a sunny day.

So Allie had done the only thing she could to make sure Mel would never hear AJ's slanderous singing. She'd faked a sore throat and texted Mel with the bad news, asking him if he could come take care of her. Luckily, he'd agreed.

Her hair ninety percent dry, Allie headed up the spiral staircase and into the Jackie O bedroom. After throwing on a shiny set of gold pj's, she crawled into her bed and assumed the illin' position. Under three blankets and propped up on five pillows, Allie turned to stare moodily at AJ's bed, just two beds away from her own. It was unmade, with bunched-up blankets swirled in a pile in the center, its edges messily strewn with clothes and bottles of high-end organic moisturizer. Allie unwrapped her comforter and stood up, suddenly filled with righteous annoyance. *If you want to clean the planet, maybe you should start with your bed!*

Allie couldn't stand looking at AJ's disorganized mess another second. If she was stuck home all night, at least she could be stuck in a clean room. Shaking her head at the injustice of tidying up her enemy's gross stuff, Allie headed toward AJ's bed and started picking up after the singing slob.

"Eeek!" Allie shrieked in terror.

AJ's comforter had moved! Did AJ have mice? Had she adopted a wild ferret and left it to fester in her bed while she went on the Muse Cruise? Allie didn't want to find out, but she couldn't just let vermin hang out two beds away from her. She gingerly pinched the edge of the covers between two fingers and quickly peeled it back from AJ's mascara and foundation–smeared sheets.

"Oh! Sorry!" Allie put her hand to her mouth and dropped the covers—underneath them was no ferret. It was AJ herself, curled up in a tight ball, and looking even paler than usual. "I thought you were vermin."

"Ugghh," AJ groaned, pulling the comforter down around her neck. Her face was damp with sweat and whiter than Casper the Friendly Ghost. "I have brutal cramps. I can't move." AJ's forest-green eyes focused on Allie's and filled with tears, sending an unwelcome twinge of sympathy through her stomach.

Allie flashed AJ a pity-frown and furrowed her forehead as if she was deeply concerned for the songstress' welfare. "That sucks, AJ. What about the cruise?" She gave herself an internal round of applause for playing the role of concerned roomie to perfection.

"I can't go," AJ moaned, rolling her eyes back in her

head from pain or annoyance or both. "I can't even move! It's like knives are stabbing my stomach. I even recorded three new songs so that everyone could download them onto their aPods! I've been prepping for weeks!"

Did AJ really think Allie would be sympathetic to the fact that she couldn't spread her slander at the cruise? "Tragic," she said finally, shaking her head.

A moment later, as AJ went back to moaning and clutching her belly, a brilliant idea washed up on the shore of her mind. AJ wasn't going to sing at the cruise, but maybe someone else could. . . .

Allie ran to the bathroom and grabbed some Motrin, along with a handful of the homeopathic melatonin pills Skye swore cured insomnia instantly. She filled a beaker with filtered water and brought all of it to AJ's bedside, channeling Nurse Nightingale.

"Here, sweetie, take this. It's Motrin and homeopathic menstrual management pills. Should help with your cramps." *And put you to sleep.*

AJ sat up in bed, weakly reaching for the water and downing all the pills without even looking at Allie. "Thanks," she murmured, collapsing back onto her pillows. She was used to being waited on, Allie reminded herself. After all, the girl had been a huge star for the past three years. At that point, you took everyone's kindness for granted. At least, that's what Allie hoped for.

"I'll tell the muses you aren't feeling well. If you want, I could bring your music and we could play it on the boat. That way, it'll be kind of like you're there, even though you're here." Allie smiled brightly at AJ and tried to look like she didn't care if AJ said yes.

AJ rubbed her eyes, then clutched her midsection with both tiny, scraggly hands. "Good idea," she grunted. "Tell people all the songs are available to download. Give me your aPod—I'll synch it with mine." Allie handed her phone to the green meanie, her stomach cartwheeling at how easy AJ was making this.

AJ hunched over the phone for a minute, then put it into Allie's waiting palm. "Thanks."

"No problem," Allie said. "I'll make sure they play it." *Just like I'm playing you.*

"You're the best," AJ said. "Sorry about all those songs I wrote about you. It's all, you know, just part of my creative journey. I had to hate you so I could write the songs." AJ's black hair fanned over her white pillowcase. Smiling up at Allie, she looked like a gothic princess suffering from tuberculosis.

Allie almost pitied her.

But not quite.

In fact, not at all. Definitely not enough to rethink her plan.

"Oh, totally. I get it," Allie replied breezily, turning away from AJ and rolling her eyes. She needed to get dressed quick and get out of here if she was going to intercept Mel and make it onto the boat. "You just rest now. Try to sleep."

"Thanks," AJ turned over and moaned into her pillow before pulling her comforter back up over her head, high enough to cover her tangled mass of black hair. Not having time to wait for AJ to fall into a homeopathically enhanced sleep, Allie raced silently around the Jackie O bedroom, throwing on a stretchy silver minidress and an easily-ditched pair of mary janes. She quickly glossed her lips and lined her eyes in silver, and at the last second decided to dab on a few drops of AJ's lavender essential oil. She smiled at her reflection in the mirror, wishing she had time to primp a bit more. But her natural radiance would have to be enough for tonight—she didn't have time for an elaborate home make-over. Allie pulled her blond hair into a high pony and threw in a pair of blue chandelier earrings to bring out her eyes.

Back in the bedroom, Allie shot a quick glance at AJ's bed and silently cheered when she heard snoring coming from under the pile of blankets. *Out cold!* Next, she tiptoed to AJ's closet and slid the door open with one finger. Her smile widened as she spotted what she was looking for: AJ's acoustic guitar, a crocheted green tam and one of her white cotton thrift-store sack dresses. Giddy with excitement and anticipation, Allie grabbed the goodies and took off down the spiral staircase, not daring to look back. She bolted out the door of Jackie O and didn't stop until she was halfway to the dock.

Panting, her hands shaking, she sent Mel a text.

Allie: Change of plans—I made a miraculous recovery. Meet me at the dock—time to cruise!

Allie's mind raced even faster than her legs pumping toward the Muse Cruise. If tonight was anything like she hoped, Allie might achieve two impossible feats—she'd lock lips with Mel, beating out all the other Alphas in the contest to win the eldest Brazille brother, and she'd finally get AJ back for her musical hate-fest. After tonight, everything wrong in Allie's life might suddenly be right.

Allie had one final, breathless thought before she reached the dock, running with AJ's guitar clattering against her back and her huge tote bag swinging from her arm. She was finally becoming a true Alpha—ruthless, talented, and willing to do whatever it took to claw her way up the social ladder.

21

"Attention, Alphas," a breezy female voice smoother than the sea they floated on wafted out from the cruise ship's speakers. "The first annual Muse Cruise will set sail in five minutes."

Charlie's mocha-brown eyes scanned the crowd as she clutched her Heartbreak Helper helmet close to her chest. She shivered in her shiny brown bandeau top she'd paired with capris, wishing she'd brought a sweater. All along the railing of the A-shaped ship, muses from each dorm stood dispensing words of inspiration and wisdom. Each muse wore a couture gown inspired by women of the ages. There were 1920s Dior flapper muses, nineteenth-century muses with towering hairstyles and corseted gowns, 1980s punk princess muses, and even some muses in ultra-futuristic gowns from this year's runway shows. Thalia wore an Alexander McQueen gown that looked like the love child of the

157

Eiffel Tower and a mirrored disco ball. Her golden tresses had been teased and lacquered into a romantic faux-hawk studded with silver-and-black rosebuds, and her eyes shone from the center of a thick stripe of silvery paint.

Charlie's arms ached with the weight of her Heartbreak Helper, and she wondered if it had been a bad idea to bring it on the cruise. Lugging it around was annoying, but word of her invention had spread faster than a Malibu brushfire and everyone seemed desperate to try it for themselves. Apparently, there were a lot more broken hearts on Alpha Island than just Charlie's.

"And that's why we need to press on, even when adversity strikes," Thalia was saying as Charlie approached the circle surrounding the muse. She wiped a grain of sushi rice from her neon-pink lips. "Because we only go around once."

"That we know of," Hannah Hesse interrupted. "One of us might discover proof of reincarnation. You never know."

Thalia nodded thoughtfully. "Maybe so," she said, her golden eyes crinkling as she pondered the idea. "What do you think, Charlie? As an inventor and scientist, do you think our souls inhabit other bodies after we die?"

Charlie blushed and shrugged. She was too focused on bouncing back from her fight with Darwin to focus on the afterlife. "I hope so. I could use a second chance."

"Second chances come when we least expect them,"

Thalia said lightly. "Excuse me, girls, I need to meet with the other muses to put the finishing touches on tonight's entertainment."

When Thalia had glided away, a train of silver triangles trailing behind her, Hannah turned to face Charlie. The tiny stud in her nose caught the last rays of the setting sun, and Charlie noticed that Hannah's eyes were shiny with tears. "Can I give the Heartbreak Helper a try?" she asked, her voice cracking.

"Sure," said Charlie, pulling a deck chair over to Hannah and motioning for her to sit down. "Who broke your heart?"

Hannah sighed and swatted at the corners of her eyes. "Dingo keeps running away every time I get close. I think I scared him when I slipped a love letter into his cereal at breakfast."

Charlie instructed Hannah to close her eyes and carefully put the helmet over her spiky red-black hair. In seconds, a group of heartbroken girls gathered around them, each clamoring for a turn.

Celia De La Cruz waved her hand in Charlie's face. "Me next, okay? I can't sleep, I'm so heartbroken. Taz gave all six Oprahs the same line about us being special and unique. He played us all!" Celia wailed. "I hate boys!"

"Okay, you're next," Charlie said. *Sounds like Taz to me,* she thought. This was all Shira's fault. What kind of person brings one hundred beautiful girls to an island with only five boys?

"My turn next!" a few girls shouted and began shoving to get close to the Heartbreak Helper. "No, me!"

Gabriella Santz, an A-list producer's daughter and would-be architect whose eyes were swollen with fresh heartache, pushed her way to the front of the crowd. "Mel ditched me after I mentioned I didn't like *The Proposal.* I tried to tell him it was because I was on set during the filming so I couldn't get into it, but he said he didn't want to listen to a rom-com hater!"

Charlie sigh-nodded. It was going to be a long night. Almost every Alpha had a sob story and a broken heart to go with it. She wasn't sure tangerine mist and a smile was going to cut it—what they needed was distraction. And more boys! But unless Shira became a different person, more boys weren't likely to materialize.

"I think it helped," Hannah said, handing the helmet back to Charlie and wiping tangerine essence off her upper lip. "Thanks."

"No problem," Charlie muttered. "Next!"

Even if Charlie could heal the heartbreak of all these girls, she couldn't fix her own. Her helmet helped, but only a little. Tears still stung her eyes every time she thought about Darwin. Even though she hadn't seen him since their fight in the PAP, she felt him hovering by her side like a phantom limb. Her memories of him were everywhere, and yet he was nowhere to be found.

As Celia grunted inside the helmet, Charlie scanned the ship's deck again, hoping to stumble into the path of Darwin's hazel gaze. But instead of locking eyes with Darwin, she spotted Allie, smiling and giggling next to the railing of the ship about twenty feet away, leaning her head on . . . *no way.*

Allie's head rested on Mel's bulky, blazered shoulder.

Charlie laughed out loud, clapping her hands together like it was Christmas morning and she'd just opened the ultimate present. This time, she didn't need the help of her heartbreak helmet to force her lips into a smile. "You have another minute, then show the next girl how to use the helmet," she instructed Celia before pushing her way through the lovelorn line toward Allie and Mel, who were cuddling closer than conjoined twins.

Had Charlie's crazy plan actually worked? Skidding to a stop on the deck in front of Allie, Charlie was desperate for dirt. "Hi," she sang out. Allie wiggled her fingers and grinned back. Her cheeks were flushed and her navy blue eyes looked brighter than Charlie had ever seen them. "Can I talk to you for a sec? Over there?" Charlie chin-thrust in the direction of the ship's railing, made up of interlocking golden A's.

"Hi, Charlie." Mel smiled.

"Hi," Charlie said, grabbing Allie's hand and pulling insistently. "Be right back, okay?"

Mel nodded. "Bye, babe!"

"What happened?" Charlie whisper-smiled when they reached the rail. "Are you guys . . . together?"

"I think so," Allie sigh-smiled. "We ran into each other on the track last night. We have a real connection. I've been wanting to tell you about it all day! You were right, Charlie. From now on I'll totally listen to you about everything."

"I'm so happy for you guys," she gushed. *And so happy for me!* Charlie's heart flip-soared like a Cirque du Soleil acrobat. But then her acrobat faltered for a second. She couldn't just assume Darwin would take her back. . . .

"What about you?" Allie's forehead wrinkled and she put a hand on Charlie's shoulder.

Charlie looked down and studied the varnished wooden boards of the ship's deck, trying to ignore the roar of her heartbeat thrumming in her ears. "What *about* me?" she managed.

"You were right about me and Mel, which means you knew things with Darwin . . ." Allie's voice rose with pinched emotion.

Charlie held her breath and looked into her friend's eyes. Had Allie figured out her plan to get back together with Darwin?

"It was never gonna happen between me and Darwin," Allie continued. "And we both know why."

"We do?" Charlie squeaked.

Allie flashed Charlie a rueful smile. "I never stood a chance, because Darwin loves *you*. Maybe you should give things with him another shot." Allie widened her eyes and pointed at the plank connecting the ship to the dock. "Here he comes."

Charlie's thoughts ping-ponged from hope to fear and back again. She took a deep breath and stuck her hand into the air, waving wildly at Darwin as he boarded the ship. He wore a white linen blazer over a deep green T-shirt, a straw fedora balanced jauntily on his light brown waves. *White for a truce, green for new beginnings.* Charlie blinked hard, her breath caught in her throat. Looking at Darwin's tan skin glowing in the twilight, her attraction to him was suddenly as sharp as a knife in her throat. Now that her Allie agony was a thing of the past, Darwin wasn't off-limits anymore, which meant the feelings she'd been working so hard to suppress revved inside her like a motorcycle's engine.

Her stomach clenched as Darwin spotted her hand and followed it down to her face. His mouth squeezed into a determined frown, he began to weave his way through the crowd and walk in their direction. She pushed her way through the ship's crowded deck and walked toward him, conflicting waves of terror and excitement washing over her with each step.

Now that she could finally open up to him and start over, would he stonewall her and send her heart farther into the abyss, or would he consider taking her back? To be this close to potential happiness was almost too much to bear.

Pushing past throngs of dressed-up Alphas, Charlie's eyes remained locked with Darwin's as if connected by an invisible rope.

The rope's pull was so strong that Charlie nearly crashed into Yvette, who stepped in front of Charlie and extended her sinewy arms to give her fellow IM a hug. "Congrats," Yvette squeaked, motioning over her shoulder at the cluster of girls still surrounding Charlie's Heartbreak Helper. "Your helmet is a hit. I wish I'd thought of it."

"Thanks," Charlie said, dying to get away from Yvette. "You can have it. I don't need it anymore."

"Are you serious?" Yvette squealed.

"It's all yours." Charlie pushed her way gently around Yvette and a few lingering girls until she got to where Darwin stood, arms folded, waiting for her.

"Something to say?" he said coolly. Inhaling his cinnamon-and-saltwater smell, Charlie practically swooned.

"Let's go inside," Charlie breathed, her heart beating in her throat. Her feelings for him were more powerful than ever—she was more nervous around him now than she'd been the first time they'd kissed. She grabbed Darwin's sweatshirt-clad arm and pulled him along the deck until she found a door marked MAINTENANCE. It would have to do.

Charlie jiggled the doorknob for a moment, then hurled her shoulder against the door until it swung open. Spying a string hanging from a bare bulb on the ceiling, she reached up and yanked it, then shut the door behind them.

"Planning to interrogate me?"

The closet's bare bulb swung ominously above them. The ship's horn honked once and its engine groaned to life. The cruise had begun. Charlie remembered learning that once a boat sailed three hundred feet into the ocean it was in international waters, where different laws applied. She stared into Darwin's adorable face and hoped that maybe different emotional laws might also apply at sea. Maybe in the water, they might have a real chance again.

She took a deep breath, grabbing a mop handle for moral support and to keep from falling into Darwin as the ship set sail. "I'm sorry, D. For letting your mom dictate our relationship. And for letting my friendship with Allie get in the way. And I don't blame you for hating me enough to drop me off in the jungle, alone." She paused, her coffee-brown eyes searching his hazel ones.

He took off his straw fedora and nodded slowly, a light brown curl falling across his forehead. Charlie wanted to brush it aside, but she didn't dare. No trace of a smile played on his kissable lips, no twitch of his dimpled cheek gave him away. *What is he thinking?* For once, Charlie couldn't read Darwin's mind. It was as if he'd slid a heavy velvet curtain over his emotions. She wondered if she would ever be allowed to peek behind the curtain again.

Charlie cleared her throat and continued. "My whole life, I've been part of your family's entourage. I think I needed this time apart to know I could stand on my own, be my own person. But once I saw I could do that, I realized that a huge part of who I was—was your soul mate." *Am I still your soul mate?* Charlie's eyes filled with tears. Why wasn't Darwin saying anything? He stood there, blinking, watching her impassively, the way Simon Cowell watched wannabes audition for *Idol.*

Charlie groped for the right words to say next and wiped a runaway tear away as it traced a path down her cheek. "I'm ready to be with you again. Completely. And I promise, nobody else will ever be in charge of us."

A puff of air shot out of Darwin's nostrils. The cleaning products clanked around in the closet.

It was so quiet, Charlie could hear the water lapping the bottom of the ship beneath the hum of the engine. But Darwin didn't move to fill the tense silence with words. Had he lost his voice? Was he trying to decide how to tell her they were over? Charlie's face went hot with anticipation.

"Darwin?" she said in a strangled voice, reaching out for

his hand. She squeezed his fingers in hers, her throat filling with cottony dread. A terrified ache began to form in her chest. If Darwin turned her down now, she didn't want to think about continuing to live on the same island with him. The pain would be too much to bear, the thought of him with another Alpha too impossible to fathom. . . .

But then Darwin's grip tightened. His lips lifted into a smile that filled his whole face. "Are you going to say please?"

Relief mingled with joy washed over Charlie, opening up the floodgates of her heart and releasing a torrent of happy tears. She pulled him to her and nuzzled her face into his sweatshirt, soaking the fabric.

"Please! Please!" she laughed, shivering in anticipation of being engulfed in one of Darwin's bear hugs again. She lifted her face up to meet his, and he leaned in. Soon, their lips locked as if for the first time. The kiss was electrifying—a bolt of lightning hot enough to melt an iceberg. Charlie's knees wobbled as Darwin wrapped his strong arms around her shoulders. She felt lighter than air, giddy and amazed, as if she had arrived home after a long journey and discovered that her house had been beautifully remodeled. Charlie's heart sang an aria as Darwin's kiss told her everything she needed to know.

22

ALPHA OCEAN
MUSE CRUISE
FRIDAY, OCTOBER 8TH
7:32 P.M.

Skye rested a hand on the interlocking golden A's that formed the ship's railing and executed a few celebratory pliés, smiling as the party headed out to sea. She couldn't help it—even when she didn't want to think about dance, her body automatically went there. She swept one arm into the air in a graceful arabesque and turned away from the rapidly receding island. Everywhere she looked, dressed-up girls laughed and danced along with gorgeous muses in museum-worthy outfits. The Black Eyed Peas' "Imma Be" blasted from the ship's portal-shaped speakers, and Skye's hips twitched to the beat. She channeled Fergie and shimmied along the railing, feeling free for the first time in ages. Dancing at the Muse Cruise instead of in Triple's boot camp was the gift that kept on giving.

A four-foot-high robot shaped like a man's torso rolled up next to her and beep-listed the contents of the tray balanced on top of it: "Porcini-crusted short rib spring rolls. Beep! Hamachi jalapeño roll. Beep! Avocado, shrimp, and mango salad cups."

"Yum," Skye giggled, snagging one of everything and popping all of it in her mouth. She smile-chewed and turned to give Triple an excited hug. "Tell me you love me."

"Okay, Katy Perry. Simmer down," Triple said.

In spite of Triple's perma-pout, Skye knew it had been the right move for both of them to come tonight. A full moon rose in the sky and lit up the faux-cean, turning it from deep blue to silver as the night darkened, and they had already spotted two dolphins frolicking in the deep as they hurriedly boarded the ship. On the boat, inspiring holographic quotes beamed in neon pink and shimmery gold onto the ship's A-shaped glass walls. The food was to die for, the music was killer and current, and the muses were dressed to impress. The whole evening was totally inspirational, and if there was one thing Skye needed tomorrow when she performed the routine for Mimi, it was inspiration.

All week, she and Triple had been excused from dance class, holed up in llama pens, the jungle, the lake, an obstacle course behind the café involving giant banana cream pies, and a lot of other places Skye wished she could forget. Now, tonight, they were finally going to have some fun. She spotted Allie and Mel on the other side of the boat cabin, standing close together and gazing out to sea. *Aw!*

Skye sniffed the air, savoring the ocean smell mingling with Triple's Chanel No. 19 and Skye's own perfume: Body Shop White Musk eau de toilette—a scent she sometimes wore to remind herself that not so long ago, she'd been a twelve-year-old at the White Plains Mall, buying her first bottle of perfume without her mother's input. Bringing her forearm to her nose and inhaling the musky vanilla scent, Skye was instantly comforted by the tiny trace of her old, pre-Alphas existence.

Until the sound of the Trapezoid twins' screechy voices snapped her out of it.

"Limbo contest!" their two sets of glitter-glossed mouths yelled from inside the ship's cabin, turning Skye's heart from muscle to glass. She looked inside and saw Taz surrounded by a mob of Alphas. Tiffany Thompson brandished a broom handle and attempted a Beyoncé-style booty-shake. "The prize is a kiss from Taz!"

Her face hot with fury and envy, Skye grabbed Triple's wrist and pulled her toward the dance floor. The Peas had faded out and now Ke$ha's "Tik Tok" rushed through the speakers. Inside the glass-walled ship, Alphas shimmied in line for the limbo.

Skye noticed Seraphina and Syd curled up on a couch in the corner of the room feeding each other sashimi. Then Skye's teal eyes found Taz. He stood to one side of the chaotic group of girls and presided over the limbo contest, his shoulders bobbing slightly to the beat. He wore a black tux jacket over jeans and an untucked white V-neck T-shirt. His black hair shone blue in the moonlight, and his blue eyes twinkled like diamonds. Skye ignored the eager Alphas surrounding him and let herself imagine the impossible. After all, she'd been a founding member of the DSL daters—she'd been making fast connections with boys since the seventh grade.

She danced a little closer to the group, letting the beat pull her toward the object of her attraction. Aiming her gaze at Taz, a confident smile masking her longing, Skye decided to give flirting with Taz the ten-second test.

"One mississppi, two Mississippi . . ." *Ohmuhgud.* She stopped counting under her breath when Taz's deep-set eyes glided toward her like blue pool balls, stopping when they landed on her gaze.

She stood up straighter and fluffed her blond wavelets, smiling at Taz and trying to project an air of positivity. She hoped her eyes said available and interested, not desperate and obsessive. But Skye's smile fell when she saw an uncomfortable, awkward-looking blush blooming across Taz's neck and face. His thick eyebrows rose and his mouth formed an embarrassed, goofy smile that shot like a flaming arrow through Skye's chest. *Ohmuhgud, he still likes me!*

But just as Skye was about to pirouette her way over to the most outgoing of all the Brazille Boys, Taz's smile morphed into a hurt-looking scowl. A moment later, looking embarrassed, he broke eye contact and looked at the floor, turning Skye's warmly beating heart cold. Then he whirled around on the dance floor, turning his back on Skye, swallowed up in seconds by the throbbing mass of Alphas on the dance floor.

Swallowing hard, Skye headed back toward the deck, remembering Triple. She found her standing alone by the railing, gazing at clusters of Alphas and muses talking and laughing in small groups.

"I think this was a mistake," murmured Triple. Turning to study her frenemy's perfect blow-out, her gorgeous gold wrap dress above mile-long legs, and a jaw line sharp enough to cut diamonds, Skye looked at Triple's eyes and should have seen confidence. Instead, she saw nerves. Triple, the girl who was so confident on the stage, who was acing every class, didn't know what to do at a party. Skye searched the deck—she was going to teach Trip how to shoot her party gun. All they needed was some target practice.

Bingo. Skye's gaze landed on Dingo, standing ten feet away on the deck, chatting with an easily ditched Alpha named Janeen, a shy girl from Kentucky who was into gardening. *Perfect.*

"Time to practice flirting, Trip." She tightened her fingers around Triple's slim wrist and sashayed away from the dance party and over to the strawberry-blond Dingo.

"Let go of me," hissed Triple, trying to shake herself free of Skye's grip. "I was fine where we were."

But by the time Skye let go of Triple's arm, they were standing in front of Dingo and Janeen. Skye let go and put a friendly hand on Triple's back, pushing her forward. "Dingo, hey. Have you met Triple?"

When Dingo smiled, he looked like a cuter version of Prince Harry. "Nice to meet you."

Skye leaned in and whispered to Janeen, whose black hair and pale skin were offset against a shimmery blue tank. She needed to ditch the smitten Southerner. "Can you go find us some chicken satay? It's Dingo's fave."

"Be right back," she whispered, giving the three of them a shy wave.

Too bad there wasn't any chicken satay at this party.

Skye leaned in and motioned to Triple, wiggling her eyebrows in a silent command that meant *do what I do*.

Tugging at her cowl-neck top, Skye casually exposed a toned shoulder and aimed it at Dingo. Triple yanked some more shoulder free of her own dress, and Skye grinned. She was learning! "Eye contact, touch his arm, laugh!" she whisper-commanded in Triple's ear. She needed to get the ball rolling.

"Hey Dingo, what do you think of Syd's new girlfriend?"

Dingo shot a look inside the glass-walled cabin of the boat. Sure enough, Syd and Seraphina were wrapped around one another more tightly than bandages on wounds. And speaking of wounds, they were both crying. Again.

"Uh," Dingo started, "I guess she's okay, when she's not crying."

"Ha! Ha! Ha!" Triple's forced laughter sounded more like a dog barking at a mailman than a girl flirting with a boy. Skye cringed. She'd finally found the Achilles' heel on Triple's ballet slipper: boys.

Triple batted her Lancôme'd lashes at Dingo, her exposed shoulder wiggling free of fabric like a molting snake.

Skye reached behind Triple's back and tugged on her blow-out. "Laugh when he makes a *joke*!" she whispered, hoping Dingo couldn't hear her over the music.

"Ow!" Triple shot her a hate-stare and rubbed her scalp.

"Hey Trip," Skye tried, "tell Dingo about our week of boot camp."

"Oh, right," Trip said, swallowing her robo-laugh and launching into the highlight reel for Dingo. She did better when she was in control, Skye realized.

Skye's attention drifted off, her eyes drawn as if by a magnetic force back to the windows of the boat's cabin, where a line of fifteen booty-shaking Alphas formed behind a limbo stick with Taz, who now stood on a chair like a lion tamer. For now, she didn't have a master plan to get Taz back, but if Skye had learned anything about herself this week, it was that she didn't go down without a fight.

". . . And that's when the bucket of worms fell from the ceiling!" Dingo was saying, and a real laugh came pouring melodically out of Trip's glossed mouth. Skye raised her platinum brows at the two of them—maybe Trip was getting the hang of flirting after all. She turned back to glance once more at Taz in the boat cabin, but instead of Taz, her attention was hijacked by the sight of Mimi walking through the dance floor and headed their way.

Yikes! What was Mimi doing here?

Skye squeezed Triple's bare arm, hard.

Triple screeched, then jumped. "Chill, lady!"

Skye flashed a micro-smile at Dingo. "We have to go. Now," she said, and began pulling Triple away.

Triple swatted at Skye, her nails grazing Skye's arms. "Stop! I'm having fun."

"Mimi alert! Shut up and walk!" Skye whispered, and without another word Triple followed her around the deck of the ship to the other side of the cabin. They ducked down behind a covered lifeboat and peered at Mimi through two sets of windows.

Mimi wore a tomato-red halter dress and a gardenia in her hair, and stood chatting with a muse just a few feet from where they'd been talking to Dingo.

"Why is she here?" whisper-yelled Skye. "I thought this was a cruise for us, not her."

"She's probably here looking for us!" Triple screeched. "She must have known we'd come."

Skye ordered her heart to beat slower so she could come up with a plan. Mimi looked relaxed and happy as she chatted with a couple of muses. Skye and Triple were obviously far from her mind. "Look at her. She's here to have a good time."

"No, *you're* here to have a good time. I cannot believe I listened to you. We should have stayed home. Now we're trapped," Triple hissed, winding her blow-out into a knotted bun, the default safety hairstyle for dancers under stress.

"We're not trapped, and we're not getting caught. I just need to think." Skye turned back to Mimi, who had finished her sushi and now strode across the deck, heading toward them. Skye's blond wavelets blew around in the ocean air as she searched frantically for an exit strategy.

"She's coming. We need to split up!" Triple whisper-screamed, her eyes wide. "I'm going into the cabin."

"We need to jump," Skye told her. It was the only answer.

"No way. If we jump, they'll see the splashing, and we'll both be history. And if they don't catch us, we'll drown before we make it to shore. The dance floor is the best option."

Skye shook her head. She'd listened to Triple about dance because, according to Mimi, she was the expert. So why wouldn't Triple listen to Skye about this? Skye had planned more parties and escaped from more teachers than anyone on Alpha Island. "Listen to me on this, Trip. I know what I'm doing. It's a short swim, and the water is warm." She frowned at Triple. She wasn't going to beg.

"The only person I listen to is myself," Triple spat, glaring at Skye and crossing her arms. Meanwhile, Mimi strode around the deck, getting closer with each mincing step of her three-inch stilettos.

"Fine. Your loss," said Skye, struggling to keep the hurt out of her voice.

Without another word, Triple stood up and strode confidently inside toward the dance party. Skye shook her head and glanced toward Mimi, who ambled obliviously around the deck, headed toward where Skye crouched.

Skye pulled off her slouchy silver top and crawled over to the railing, peering out across the water to the shore. She took a deep breath. The Pavilion and its brise-soleil wings were just a five-minute swim away, she told herself. Five minutes of swimming through Shira's bathwater-warm sea would be fun, maybe even refreshing. In just her leo and leggings, she was practically in a bathing suit.

Then, in one fluid motion, she vaulted over the railing, pushed off from the side of the ship, and jumped into the water far below. Surfacing after her jump, Skye paddled through the gentle silvery waves toward the shore under the light of the full moon. She looked up at the boat just once, squinting to make sure a crowd hadn't assembled at the railing, but the party raged on. Skye smiled. Triple would have to hide from Mimi all evening, but Skye had the ocean all to herself.

Pausing to float on her back and catch her breath, Skye stared up at the moon. Then she smiled, as if only the two of them were in on the joke. After all, what she'd said to Triple was true: She *always* made a splash at parties.

23

In the glass-walled cabin of the A-shaped ship, Allie tried to ignore the jealous stares of the other Alphas on the dance floor as she and Mel swayed to Taylor Swift's "You Belong with Me." She tried to focus on Mel's strong arms around her, on the smell of his cologne and the feeling of his blond hair grazing her forehead, but she was too busy worrying to fully enjoy it.

Nervous energy shot through her limbs as she mentally walked through her plan again and again. She was so anxious that a moment ago she'd hallucinated a blond girl in a black leotard and leggings jumping over the ship's railing. She rubbed her eyes and shook her ponytail, blinking at the spot she thought she'd seen the jumper. Taking a deep breath of Mel's woodsy scent, she pulled away from him and looked into his broad face.

Channeling confidence she wasn't feeling and project-

179

ing calmness she desperately wanted, she winked at Mel and cocked her head playfully to one side. "I have to run to the little Alphas' room," she purred.

"Okay," he said, and grinned. "I'll grab us another plate of sushi."

"I might be a little while," Allie added hastily, rolling her eyes and chuckling weakly, hoping she sounded believable. "Girl talk. It's like a gossip convention in that bathroom." She turned away from Mel and walked through the dancing crowd, stopping only to swipe her tote bag from the back of a chair.

Luckily, the bathroom convention she'd made up was nowhere in sight. Allie breathed a sigh of relief at finding the huge bathroom empty, then quickly darted into a stall. The walls of the bathroom stall were covered with ancient-looking pirate maps, complete with X's marking the spot for buried treasure, and the door featured a holographic map of the ship's course around the island, with a blinking blue A showing where the party was right now.

Telling herself not to waste time checking out the décor, Allie yanked her silver minidress up over her head. With any luck, AJ's album would soon be buried like pirate's treasure, along with her reputation. Shivering in her bra and underwear, Allie tried not to breathe as she carefully slipped AJ's vintage white dress over her head. When Allie finally took a breath, she smelled lavender and the thrift-store reek of dead people. *Perfect—AJ's signature scent.*

Next, Allie found AJ's crocheted green tam and shoved it over her honey-blond hair, stuffing her ponytail inside and pulling it down low on her forehead. Hiding her shoes behind the toilet, Allie unlocked the stall door and ran toward a row of gilt-framed mirrors above the long row of sinks. Opening her bag again, she took out sunglasses and an eyeliner pencil. She expertly drew AJ's mole onto her upper lip. The one good thing about sneaking into the Academy by posing as AJ was that she could reclaim her fake identity in her sleep. Adding sunglasses made her transformation complete. Nobody would know the eyes underneath the glasses were blue, not green. Examining the AJ facsimile staring back at her in the mirror, Allie slouched the way AJ always did. She smiled and tried out AJ's high, breathy voice on her reflection. "Welcome back."

Hurrying out of the bathroom just as a couple of Alphas came in, Allie ditched her tote in the wings of the cabin's small stage and grabbed AJ's guitar. She slouched over to Thalia, pulling her tam lower on her forehead in a fit of hair-anoia.

"AJ!" Thalia smiled, reaching up to pat a couple of the silver rosebuds in her giant faux-hawk. Allie felt bad lying to

Thalia, but she had no choice: Thalia was MC'ing tonight. "Are you ready to go on?"

Allie nodded and smiled at Thalia with her mouth closed, a knife of guilt stabbing her chest.

Allie-as-AJ followed the train of Thalia's Eiffel Tower dress and waited while Thalia turned the music off and took the mic. While Thalia welcomed everyone to the first annual Muse Cruise and started talking about how inspiring it was to be with so many extraordinary girls, Allie tuned out. Spotting the soundboard, she quickly plugged her aPod into one of the output cords. Everything in place, she darted out from the wings and pasted on her best AJ-about-to-sing smile.

Allie had thought through her plan carefully, but there was one thing she wasn't prepped for. Being up onstage felt ah-mazing! She let the adoration wash over her, using the ego boost to fuel her courage to go through with the plan. But when she looked at the crowd more carefully, she noticed that almost everyone—everyone but Charlie, Darwin, Mel, and Triple—was making the official Identity Theft symbol, first raising their index fingers to create the I, then crossing it with their other hand to form the T. The crowd was in total solidarity with AJ—and totally anti-Allie, the identity thief who inspired the lyrics.

Allie held AJ's guitar in front of her like a shield and blinked away the tears of terror that had sprung into her eyes. Her heartbeat moved from a trot to a gallop, and the adoring crowd in front of her suddenly seemed dangerously close to an angry mob. But just as she started to consider running offstage, her aPod cued up "Identity Theft." Now she had no choice but to go ahead with her plan, which, she now saw, had seemed a lot easier from the safety of the bathroom stall.

You can do this, Al. She took a deep breath and began fake-strumming AJ's guitar in time with the music, her eyes glued to Mel's face. She could do this, for him. For herself. Instead of letting the audience's hatred wound her like poison darts, she would use it as fuel. She would channel it into revenge on AJ.

Allie played along with the song, her fingers expertly faking each chord, her fingers strumming the guitar in ways she didn't know they could. When AJ's recorded voice started to sing, Allie grabbed the mic and lip-synched along, not missing a syllable. After a few lines, Allie unleashed her first attack. While recorded-AJ sang, onstage-AJ coughed into the mic. Coughing just once, she returned to lip-synching, shaking her head slightly and twisting her face into a mortified expression. But when Allie scanned the crowd during a guitar solo, everyone was still dancing and clapping along to the song, yelling "Stop Thief! Identity Theft!"

Nobody even noticed Allie's lip-synch giveaway!

When the chorus of the song began again, Allie

coughed louder. Harder. This time, she was determined to make people see that "AJ" wasn't really singing. She doubled over, clutching the mic to her stomach for a second as recorded-AJ kept right on singing. Then she straightened back up and continued to lip-synch as if nothing had happened.

A tide of anger rippled through the crowd. "She's lip-synching!" shouted Hannah Hesse in the front row. Allie continued to lip-synch and strum the guitar, but now she did it out of time with the music. She made herself blush and concentrated on appearing flustered.

"Sorry!" she yelled into the mic in her high AJ voice.

Soon, the entire audience erupted in booing. The crowd stopped dancing. Now everyone stood there shooting hate-daggers at Allie. Only this time, Allie thought gleefully, they were glaring at AJ. Someone yelled, "Who's the fake now?"

Allie ducked as a sandal flew threw the air and nearly hit her in the head. Her plan was officially a success! AJ's rep was destroyed, and soon people might not walk around the Academy humming "Identity Theft." It wasn't so cool anymore, now that the singer was a fake herself.

As the song ended and the crowd's booing and hissing drowned out the song's final notes, Allie-as-AJ burst into fake tears and ran offstage. *Yet another thing I know how to do from experience!* Allie giggled at the irony—her past unmasking, the most humiliating half-hour of her life, had prepared her for the role of a lifetime.

Allie ran into the wings and dove for her tote bag. Before the angry mob stormed the stage and attacked AJ, she had to get rid of her disguise. She licked her hand and wiped it across her faux-mole, then ripped off AJ's dress and hat like they were on fire. She pulled her silver minidress over her head and tugged it down, then bolted to the bathroom to grab her shoes.

A few minutes later, Allie sauntered casually across the dance floor, past clusters of indignant Alpha girls—all of them dishing about how lame AJ's performance was—to where Charlie stood with Darwin and Mel.

"What's going on?" she asked, blinking her eyes. Hopefully, her face looked as innocent and confused as an amnesiac's.

"Babe, you missed it! AJ got booed off the stage. It was actually kind of funny." Mel was so cute and so sweet, Allie nearly swooned. Those words, out of Mel's gorgeous mouth, were almost *too* perfect.

Allie brought her navy blue eyes to his violet ones. "Really? How weird. I went outside to get some air, and when I came back, her concert had ended. I was wondering why." She shrug-smiled as if to say, *oh well, life goes on*.

Inside, her heart buzzed like a hive of honeybees. Had

she really pulled off an AJ takedown *and* started hanging out with the cutest guy on the island? If this were a dream, she didn't want to wake up.

"She must be freaking out right now," Darwin said, shaking his head. "I mean, I knew she was kind of fake, but I didn't think she was the type to lip-synch a live show."

"Poor AJ. She probably had her reasons." Allie shook her head as if she sympathized with her roommate, remembering Darwin had always been a huge fan of AJ's music. Looking at him now, Allie couldn't believe she'd had such a huge crush on him only a week ago. He was just a bridge boy for her, Allie realized. A boy to get her from one serious relationship (Fletcher) to another (Mel). Allie turned to Charlie, noticing her bestie was standing very close to Darwin—and they were holding hands.

Allie's eyes moved from Charlie's hand to her face. Charlie nodded subtly, her eyes shining with happiness. Then Charlie's eyes bounced to the stage and back to Allie, and her brown eyebrows shot into the air, silently asking Allie if she'd been AJ only moments before.

Allie nodded and bit her lip, confessing all of it to Charlie in that tiny gesture. In seconds, both girls erupted into laughter. They grabbed each other's shoulders and huglaughed, twirling around, the faces of all the Alphas on the ship spinning past in a blur. Darwin and Mel looked at each other and shrugged as their girlfriends howled in hysterics.

Finally slowing their teacup spin to a stop, Allie reached up and wiped a tear from the end of Charlie's nose.

Allie sighed, looking out at the island that finally felt like home, at Mel and Darwin walking toward her with smiles on their faces, and back into Charlie's smiling coffee-brown eyes. Then she leaned in for one more hug.

24

Skye squeezed the last few drops of moisture out of her hair, flipped her head over, and wrapped a silver towel around her head like a turban. Dressed in plush gold slippers and matching cashmere robe, she was finally starting to warm up after her Olympic-caliber swim to shore. Pulling her comforter around her shoulders, she shiver-shook the last chill from her lithe body and continued telling the Jackie O's—all of whom had arrived back at the dorm while Skye was in the shower—about her wet escape.

"Swimming was the easy part. Walking home soaking wet was harder."

"Ohmuhgud. You walked all the way here with no shoes?" Allie put her hands over her mouth in horror.

"I walked to the bubble train," Skye confessed. It hadn't been too bad. Luckily, the temperature of the island at night usually hovered around seventy degrees.

The only storms they had to face came when Shira got angry.

"Still," Charlie said, giggling and shaking her head, "you risked your life to avoid getting busted. You're the Lara Croft of Jackie O."

Skye laughed. "When you've been flirting with boys as long as I have, you become a better escape artist than David Blaine. Right, Trip? You did pretty well yourself." Skye wanted to include Triple in the Muse Cruise postmortem, but the dance diva had crawled into bed and buried her nose in the giant binder they'd all received when they arrived at the Academy. Triple was thumbing through the Official Alphas Handbook like she was studying for a test.

"Yeah, all's well that ends well," Triple murmured, not meeting Skye's eyes.

"Studying Shira's bible?" Charlie asked lightly.

"Just trying to wind down and get to sleep, and this boring reading material makes me drowsy." Triple buried her face deeper in the phonebook-sized handbook with the gold, swoopy A on the cover.

Whatever, Trip. Skye shrugged it off, assuming Triple was jealous of her dramatic exit. While she was swimming, Triple was cowering on the boat. But with enough time, Triple would learn how to take more risks. *Baby steps.*

"You're the stuntwoman," Charlie continued, "and she's

the Academy Award–winning actress." She stuck a thumb out and jabbed it in Allie's direction.

"Shhh!" Allie's face turned red as she motioned to AJ's bed, where the singer snored quietly, out cold.

"Ohmuhgud, fill me in," whispered Skye, beckoning Allie closer.

Allie leapt up from her bed and sat on Skye's, followed by Charlie. "Tell her," Charlie said to Allie. "You will not believe this," she giggle-whispered to Skye.

"Does this have something to do with the texts I keep getting?" Skye pointed to her aPod. Luckily, she'd accidentally left it in its charger all evening so it didn't have to swim in the ocean with her. When she'd arrived home, her inbox was filled with photos and texts, all saying something about AJ lip-synching her performance on the Muse Cruise.

"Are they about AJ?" Allie asked, her eyes widening.

"Uh-huh."

"Then yes. That was me. Oops!" Allie shrugged her shoulders and threw her hands up in the air as if she'd dropped a glass or burned some toast instead of pulled off an enormous fake-out to get back at AJ.

"Wow." Skye unwound her towel turban and shook her platinum waves out. "She has no idea yet, does she?"

The three girls looked over at AJ, splayed out in a deep slumber, a thin line of drool spilling down her cheek, extending from her half-open mouth. Allie shook her head sadly and burst out giggling along with Charlie. Skye laughed, too—AJ was all about AJ and had never bothered to make friends with the Jackie O's. Her songs about Allie might have been catchy, but they were also mean. It was nice to imagine her getting a taste of what Allie had been going through.

Skye sank back into the pile of pillows on her bed and turned back to Allie and Charlie, when an electric flash in the sky froze the tale of her journey in her throat. Skye's panicked eyes met Charlie's brown ones, then Allie's dark blue ones. All were wide with alarm. Sudden bad weather inside the Alpha Island Biosphere could mean only one thing.

Shira was on the warpath.

A few seconds of nervous anticipation ticked by, followed by a crash of thunder that rocked the bedroom hard enough to make the lights flicker. Allie yelped like a newborn puppy, pulling her sweatshirt's hood up over her head and rolling off Skye's bed onto the floor. AJ sleep-grunted and flipped over from her back to her stomach.

"What's going on?" Skye whispered, turning to Charlie.

Charlie bit her lip and shrugged. "No idea."

"She knows!" whisper-shouted Allie, uncoiling from the fetal position and leaping back onto Skye's bed. Her eyes were coated in Shira-induced panic-tears. "I'm busted!"

Charlie shook her head. "No way. Nobody knows it was you."

Skye sat up, her spine ruler-straight, sudden fear making her scalp tingle and her ears hot. She snuck another glance at Triple, who continued to read, seemingly unaware of the weather. "Shira must have found out about my swim. I'm toast."

Skye looked around the bedroom, taking it all in—the horseshoe-cluster of beds, the glass walls, the amazing closets, and the swirly gold-and-silver carpet that warmed to the touch of cold feet. "I'll miss you guys."

Another crack of thunder ripped through the sky, ushering in a violent storm. Rain pounded down on the domed glass ceiling in ferocious, slanted sheets. Skye squeezed her eyes shut and tried to think happy thoughts, but all she could see was Shira's disembodied head kicking her out of the Academy.

Just then, the clatter of footsteps at the door reached Skye's ears. "Ohmuhgud," Allie whispered, grabbing both Skye's and Charlie's hands. The three girls formed a triangle with their hands and waited.

They stared at each other as a pair of high heels clomped up the spiral staircase. Skye held her breath. When she saw Thalia's geometric hairstyle, she exhaled in relief.

"Girls!" Thalia barked, sounding more like Drill Sergeant Triple than the calm, serene life coach Skye knew and loved. Thalia walked over to the wall and switched off the lights. "'Exhaustion is the shortest way to equality and fraternity, and liberty is added eventually by sleep.' Nietzsche. Time for bed," she added.

Allie and Charlie wordlessly obeyed Thalia's instructions. Triple snapped her enormous binder shut and put her sleep mask over her eyes, instantly looking the part of a rule-abiding Alpha.

Skye lay back and listened to the pounding of the rain, which sounded like millions of metal tacks hitting the glass ceiling above her. She reached out and grabbed her HAD slipper from her night table, fingering the purple satin as fervently as a nun clutching a rosary.

Disobeying Mimi just to watch fifteen girls do the limbo for a chance to kiss Taz was *so* not worth getting expelled. Skye made a silent promise to herself—if she survived tonight, she was going to channel her week of boot camp into a whole new lifestyle. One where dance came first, where she followed the rules and rose to the top. One that was a lot more like Triple's.

Thalia disappeared back down the stairs and into her muse quarters. A moment later, the front door of Jackie O slid open a second time. A pair of stilettos clicked on the clear glass staircase, this time sounding more like typewriter keys than horse hooves. A huge bolt of blue-white lightning lit up the turbulent rainstorm above Skye's head, lighting up the room for a split second just as Shira entered the bedroom, illuminating her wild red waves, her annoyed-looking face, and trench-coated body.

Skye clutched her HAD slipper tighter under her coverlet and squeezed her eyes shut again. Shira in Jackie O was an image straight out of Skye's nightmares. It was like Madonna at McDonald's—out of place and wrong on every level.

Shira walked crisply to the center of the horseshoe of beds, shaking rainwater off a huge folded black umbrella. A drop flew onto Skye's forehead, but she didn't dare move to wipe it off. She peered through squinted eyes at Shira's ice-blue eyes, glowing with anger in the semi-dark room. *Ohmuhgud.*

"I know you're all awake, so stop laying there like corpses," Shira spat in her Aussie accent. The girls sat up immediately—everyone but AJ, who for some reason actually seemed to be sleeping through their midnight intrusion.

"And her?" Shira asked the four girls cowering in their beds, waving a hand in AJ's direction.

After a beat of silence, Charlie bravely answered. "She's not feeling well."

"Ah. No matter." Shira nodded, pursing her brick-red lips. "Skye and Andrea, please get up and stand at the foot of your beds."

Ohmuhgud!

As if an electric shock launched her out of bed, Triple shot up like a jack-in-the box and gracefully arranged her

feet in second position at the foot of her bed. Skye tried
to catch Triple's eyes, but they were stuck to a distant tree
out the window. But even though the diva appeared to be
calmly gazing past Shira, her hands trembled at her sides.

Skye got up and trudged to the foot of her bed, forcing her legs forward. She shivered as a few drops of water
escaped her still-wet hair and dripped down her neck, and
realized she was still clutching her HAD slipper. Skye stood
close enough to Shira now to smell her Crème De La Mer
moisturizer. She concentrated on not passing out, waiting for the two worst words at the Academy to be directed
to her—*you're expelled*. The world-famous Aussie Alpha
wasn't wearing her trademark sunglasses, and her eyes followed Skye like she was an amoeba under a microscope—
something inhuman, an oddity to be studied.

"Mimi gave you both strict instructions not to go on
the Muse Cruise. You were to be rehearsing. You were to
make the most of your week together and perfect your dancing." Shira took a breath, pausing, her head swiveling from
Skye to Triple and back again, and the fist of fear tightened
around Skye's heart.

She thought of her mother's face when she heard the
news, of Natasha's beautiful, mournful Russian features collapsing in disappointment over her only daughter ruining
her chance to make it to the top as a dancer. She thought
of her father sighing with disappointment, and tears sprang

into her eyes. She thought of herself, twenty years from now, working as a ballet teacher for kindergarten girls in Westchester, her dreams discarded like a pair of ripped tights, and she swallowed hard.

She'd brought this on herself—on herself and on Triple!—all because she'd wanted a little fun. The fact that she'd ruined not just her own life but Triple's, too, made her snap out of her pity party. She needed to fight. No, she needed to something even harder than that. She needed to beg.

"Shira, please," Skye started, her voice cracking with tears. "It was all my idea . . . ," she admitted. "Triple didn't want any part of it," she added. It was the truth. If that meant she had to go home, at least she would go with her head held high.

Skye looked over at Triple, who stood tall, her eyes dry. A faint smile played on her plump lips. Thalia padded quietly up the stairs, holding a rolling suitcase in her arms. She set it down silently in front of Triple.

"Wrong bag," Triple informed her. "You meant to bring Skye's bag."

"Everything's in order, Andrea," Shira snipped. "You're going home. Skye will be staying."

"What?" Tears sprang into her gold-flecked eyes. "I don't understand!"

Neither did Skye.

"It's simple, really," Shira smiled, twirling her folded umbrella like a baton. "Shall we tell them what happened tonight?"

Looking into Shira's eyes, Triple folded like a card table, collapsing on her bed in a fit of tears. Skye's mouth fell open in a shocked O as she looked from Triple to Shira, waiting for an explanation.

Shira walked closer to Skye, nodding at Charlie and Allie, who had gotten out of bed to stand next to Skye for moral support. "Andrea was caught by Mimi on the cruise, and she did the worst thing an Alpha can do. She tattled on Skye to save herself." Shira's red hair blew off her face, as if a wind machine were permanently blowing at her. "Skye, you proved you could *improve*, that you're willing to work hard. But Andrea was unable to learn what she needed to learn, which was how to be a good friend. Backbends can be taught, but backbones cannot."

Skye, Charlie, and Allie all nodded silently, absorbing Shira's words.

"It's not fair!" Triple wailed. "I'm the best student here!"

"Life isn't fair," Shira snapped. "That's the great secret. Think about it on your PAP ride back to Chicago."

"Michigan!"

"Whatever."

Skye giggled internally. She felt lighter than a helium

197

balloon, as if she might float away. Her guilt over the Muse Cruise escapade evaporated like the steam on her morning latte.

"Well, I must be off. I have forty-seven more girls to kick out tonight," Shira sighed, flipping up the wide collar on her trench coat. "I warned them not to let boys get in the way of their studies and their friendships." She shrugged.

Skye was smiling so hard that her cheeks hurt.

"Andrea—Triple—" Thalia stepped out of the shadows of the room holding Triple's coat. It was black leather fringed in fake fur. As fake as Triple herself.

"Don't cry because it's over. Smile because it happened. Dr. Seuss." Thalia handed her the coat.

Triple shook her head, swallowing her last hiccupy sob, her blow-out clumped with the moisture of fresh tears. She grabbed her coat roughly and put it on, then picked up her suitcase and dragged it behind her, thumping each stair as she went. She held her head high—too proud or too furious to say goodbye.

"Wow," Allie whispered, filling the empty silence that had descended on them in the wake of Triple's departure. "How many girls are still here?"

Charlie pulled out her laptop and somberly began typing names into her spreadsheet. "Only thirty. But all that matters is that we're still here."

Skye laughed again. If she could survive tonight, she'd

survive anything. The odds that she would be the last Alpha standing were better than ever. She hoped Charlie and Allie would make it with her to the end.

"Look," Charlie said, pointing to the still stormy sky. The first of many PAPs traced an arc above them, headed back to wherever the girl inside had come from.

"So long," Skye whispered, climbing into bed.

Humming "I Will Survive" in honor of Sergeant Triple, Skye slipped her HAD slipper under her pillow and shut her eyes, a whisper of a smile on her lips.

25

Charlie rubbed sleep from her eyes and swallowed a spoonful of yogurt, granola, and blueberries. She and Darwin had gone hiking with Mel and Allie yesterday, and even though they ended their double date with a late-night snack of Nutella-banana crepes, Charlie still ate with the gusto of an Olympic athlete. She took another bite and smiled at Allie across the table. Her best friend held a breakfast burrito in one hand and her aPod in the other, texting Mel non-stop.

Skye plopped into an empty seat at the table, a Belgian waffle sliding around her tray like an air hockey puck. She put her tray down on the table and stretched her arms high over her head, grabbing her elbows with the opposite hands and pulling until her shoulders popped. Her platinum wavelets shone as the morning sun beamed down on them from all eight giant windows in the octagonal dining hall. Skye took a bite of her waffle and leaned back in her chair. "Quiet around here."

Skye was right; it *was* quiet. Until Shira's surprise spree on Friday, the dining hall was always packed tighter than a sardine can. Alphas would squeeze in tightly around the shiny white tables, and the sound of chatting girls filled the giant room.

Charlie looked around the dining hall, absorbing the new, subdued relaxation in the air. Now that there were only thirty Alphas left, none of the tables were full and many stood empty. The entrance to the spa beckoned to Charlie on one side of the dining hall, and on the other was the door to the assembly room. Between the two stood six different boutiques where the girls could purchase new clothes and makeup with aBucks, earned by getting A's.

Charlie hadn't set foot in the boutiques in weeks, but suddenly she hungered for something more exciting to wear than her basic Alphas uniform, her old party dresses, and her lab coveralls. After all, she was officially Darwin's girlfriend again. She might as well look the part. Even if he didn't care what she wore, feeling pretty would only add to her newfound happiness. She looked in the windows of each boutique and decided that after breakfast she would try a few things on.

Her concentration on a cute sparkly shrug was broken when Allie elbowed her in the ribs. "AJ," Allie leaned in and whispered in Charlie's ear, tipping her head to the right.

Charlie followed Allie's forehead thrust and saw AJ seated all alone at a corner table, still wearing her dingy green tam and scribbling in a notebook.

"She keeps trying to tell everyone it's a mistake since she slept through the Muse Cruise," Skye said. "But nobody's buying it. Now she's writing songs about being a misunderstood genius."

Allie sat back in her chair and picked at her cuticles. "I think I'll forgive her for lip-synching," she said, and smiled. "In a few days, she'll be a more humble person."

Charlie nodded. "Maybe you're right. I hear everyone hating you does wonders for your character."

"Mimi hating me definitely turned out to be a good thing," Skye chirped, waving to Ophelia and Tweety, who sat at a table across the room. "Working with Trip made me the best in the class."

"Doesn't hurt that Triple is gone, either," Charlie added gently.

Skye's eyes sparkled mischievously above a sly smile. "True."

AJ looked up from her notebook and caught Charlie's eyes for a second before looking back down and scrawling more lyrics. Charlie wondered if she'd ever grow to like AJ—it was hard to imagine, but you never knew. Now that she had Darwin back as a boyfriend and Allie and Skye as besties, she was open to anything.

Charlie leaned back in her chair and texted Darwin to see if he was coming to breakfast. She hadn't felt this relaxed since before the Academy opened. With only thirty girls left, the school seemed less like a shark tank and more like a school of minnows swimming peacefully toward Shira's finish line.

Alphas at the few occupied tables talked quietly among themselves. Everyone looked less haggard, less like a hamster on a wheel and more like what they were: lucky girls on an amazing island. Under the blow-outs and ponies were relaxed smiles, the faces of girls who knew they'd passed one of Shira's biggest tests.

"Attention, Alphas," the British voice of Charlie's mom intruded on Charlie's thoughts. "Please stand by for a special message."

The brise-soleil shades on the Pavilion lowered over the windows, turning the bright dining hall pitch-black. A screen lowered over each window, and suddenly Shira's face appeared in close-up on each one—giant, forbidding, and unreadable behind her dark sunglasses.

Giant-head Shira sat in a white leather passenger seat with massaging leather "fingers" extending from it. An A-shaped window next to her revealed palm trees, ferns, and the Delphi Observatory. A glass of sparkling water sat untouched in the foreground of the shot. Charlie knew that chair, the glass, and the window—Shira was broadcasting from the cabin of the Brazille Force One, her luxury Learjet.

"G'day, lollies," Eight Shiras boomed from the screens. The view of trees framed in the A-shaped window began to move. "As you can see, I'm headed to the mainland. A situation there demanded my attention, unfortunately, and I'm not sure how long I'll be gone."

Charlie's eyes met Allie's, then Skye's. Both of her besties looked excited, but Charlie knew Shira too well. This had to be another trap, test, or trick. When her eyes returned to the screens, the plane had gathered speed. Outside the window of Brazille Force One, trees whizzed past in a green-brown blur.

All eight Shiras continued. "I have good news. While I'm gone, you will discover a leader. That person, whoever she may be, will distinguish herself through her ability to be fair, to be strong, to survive. Someone with vision. This visionary Alpha will receive special privileges upon my return. For one, she will be an Alpha for life. And the rest . . ." Shira paused dramatically, a thin smile appearing on her face for a fraction of a second before vanishing. "The rest will remain a surprise. Good luck, girls."

All eight screens instantly went dark and slowly rolled up along with the brise-soleil shades, flooding the enormous room with light again.

Charlie hit SEND on her message to Darwin and put her phone in her skirt pocket. For a split second, the dining hall was quiet enough to hear a bobby pin drop.

Then Seraphina Hernandez-Rosenblatt—normally shy, sensitive, and introverted—did something out of character. She unclipped her long brown curls, shook out her hair so it was wild and full, then leapt out of her chair and climbed up on one of the tables, raising her hands high over her head like she'd just won a marathon. "Freedom!" she yelled, smiling wide and looking around the room, wiggling her thick eyebrows as if daring the other girls to embrace their new Shira-free existence.

Milliseconds later, the room burst into commotion like a cork had been popped from a bottle of champagne. Charlie looked around—there were no muses in sight, no teachers to speak of. In seconds, someone hacked the audio system in the pavilion to play the Black Eyed Peas "I Gotta Feeling."

"If you can't beat 'em . . ." Skye shrugged and jumped up to join the bun-heads in a celebratory dance-off.

Charlie and Allie watched as a few girls ran toward the boutiques and began tearing clothes off their hangers as if aBucks no longer applied.

Charlie wanted to be happy. She wanted to be free. But she also wanted to be an Alpha for life. She ran a hand uncertainly through her mahogany bangs and looked out the window, just in time to spot Brazille Force One slicing through the perfect blue sky.

Charlie's fingers itched the way they always did when she wanted to create. She needed to get to the lab. It would take a lot of thinking to come up with a way to lead this crazy Alpha crew. For one, Alphas didn't like to let others lead. That's what made them Alphas.

But there could only be one. She knew that now.

Turning in a slow circle in the middle of the chaotic room, Charlie wiggled her wrist until she heard the reassuring clank of her three cameo bracelets. She made a silent promise to herself: to rise to the top, and to do it without any of her classmates noticing. Once her leadership was secured, Charlie would make sure Shira knew all about it.

After all, she didn't come here to play. She came here to win.

Alpha Academy may be home to the best and the brightest, but the original alpha will always be Massie Block. . . .

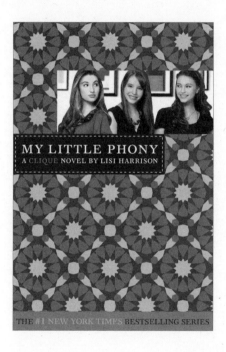

Turn the page for a peek at MY LITTLE PHONY,
A CLIQUE NOVEL by Lisi Harrison

"I love getting stoned," Massie Block sighed happily from one of the three massage tables set up in her family's barn-spa. Heated stones lay on her back, radiating warmth through her entire body like she'd just downed three soy caramel lattes.

"If we were in school right now, we'd be in third-period French," Kristen Gregory mumbled through the face hole in her massage table. The stones lined her spine like stegosaurus plates.

"*J'adore* snow days," trilled Alicia Rivera, lying on her back at the end of the row, her long, dark brown hair fanned out behind her head. Her masseuse, Amber, spritzed her with Evian mineral water.

"*Oui, oui*," Kristen agreed.

"*Woof!*" Bean chimed in from her own mini massage bed.

"Tatiana, how do you say 'snow day' in Russian?" Massie asked innocently.

"Shhhhh," hissed Tatiana. "Talking eees naht relaaacksing. Jash theenk abut a bee-yoo-ti-ful snoh-flok."

Tatiana claimed to be "frahmm RAH-shah," but Massie had a feeling her accent was about as real as Heidi Pratt's new body. Not that it mattered. Her hands were pure gold. And with all those rocks lined up on her back, Massie felt like the black diamond stretch bracelet on her Christmas list: relaxed, beautiful, and almost a million bucks.

Massie turned her head to look out the barn's sophisticated yet rustic plate-glass windows. It had snowed more than two feet the night before. The patios were dusted with shimmery powder, and the trees sparkled in the early December sun. It looked as though the MAC fairy had sprinkled pearly White Frost eye shadow over the entire Block estate and then blown it a kiss with her Sugarrimmed Dazzleglass—coated lips.

"CLAAAAAAAAAAAAAIRE!" Layne Abeley's gravelly voice boomed from outside.

"AHHHHH! I've been hit!"

CRASH!

Outside, a body slammed against the barn wall, and the spa shook. A high-pitched giggle followed.

"Eh-ma-annoying!" Massie flipped over, her heated stones tumbling to the floor. Her ex-BFF, Claire Lyons, had been squealing and giggling with her new friends all afternoon. Leave it to Claire to find the only ninth-grade girls who thought snowball fights were more fun than high school gossip. It was a total waste of an upgrade.

"Eeeen-hayel the soo-theeng ah-rom-ah," Tatiana instructed, guiding Massie back down to the table and replacing the rocks. Spicy steam startled Massie's pores as the masseuse kneaded the tension from her shoulders. But it was a lost cause. No amount of eucalyptus-infused steam could ease the pain of Claire ditching the Pretty Committee for *Layme* Abeley and two fourteen-year-old theater geeks.

Suddenly, the barn's wooden door flew open. Dylan Marvil rushed in, along with an arctic blast of air. Snowflakes speckled the back of her black cashmere coat like dandruff. Her white-mittened hands grasped the handles of a dozen brightly colored shopping bags, and her cheeks were as red as her hair.

"Where've you been?" Alicia sat up, pressing a fluffy green towel against her C-cups.

"Shooooooooooooooopppping!" Dylan burped. She set down a cardboard tray full of venti Starbucks hot chocolates and wiped her brown-stache with the back of her mitten. A cocoa-colored skid mark cut across the cashmere. "Ooops!" she shrugged. "Good thing I got a new pair. I cleaned out Neiman's, Juicy, and Michael Kors. Snow-day shopping is the best."

"Point-t-t-t," Alicia agreed through chattering teeth.

Massie pressed a button on a sleek silver remote. A second later, the electric fire in the stone fireplace ignited.

Dylan tossed her stained mittens into the hungry flames and then shook her crimson locks.

"Nice lice, Dyl!" Kristen cackled. Alicia snickered, her freshly manicured toes dangling just above the heated tile floor.

As Dylan whirled back toward them, her Brazilian blowout whipped around her face. "Don't even joke! When Megan Lambert got lice, her friends scattered like roaches in a Raid storm." She stuck her butt out to warm it in the fire's glow.

"Let's see what you got." Massie stood, and once again the pile of rocks cascaded off her warm back and crashed to the ground. Bean bolted under the glass coffee table.

"Nyyyetttttt!" Tatiana let out a yelp as one of the rocks bounced against her toe. "Off! Off!" she insisted, waving Kristen and Alicia to their feet. With a grimace, she nodded at the other masseuses, who quickly folded up their tables, packed up their oils, picked up their rocks, and followed her out into the cold afternoon.

"*Danke* very much," Massie called after them sweetly, putting on a fluffy white robe.

The three women responded by slamming the barn door shut.

"Isn't *danke* German?" Kristen giggled.

"Oh, whatevs," Massie shrugged. "They dan-kare." She padded over to Dylan's pile of bags and pulled out a baby blue cashmere hat with earflaps and tassels. It looked like something Kuh-laire would wear. With a wince, she dropped it back in the bag. "You really did buy *everything*."

"I maxed out my card," Dylan admitted. "But it was totally worth it. I got open-toed booties in faux leopard *and* faux cheetah."

"Ohhh," Alicia whine-pouted. "I'm faux jealous." Her shoulders were covered with spiderweb-like indentations from lying down on the massage table. "I can't buy anything right now. My parents told me they would send me to the Spanish Riviera for a week if I didn't shop from Thanksgiving to Christmas." She buried her nose inside Dylan's Saks bag and inhaled a Ralph Lauren sweater-coat. "Ahhhh! It's better than new puppy smell."

Bean lifted her little black head and growled.

"She was only kidding, B," Massie assured her pup, applying a coat of Pineapple Spice Glossip Girl to the pug's mouth. The pug licked it off and then sneezed. "My parents would *never* shop-block me."

"Must be nice," Kristen said with a frown.

"It is," Massie beamed.

THUNK!

THUNK!

THUNK!

Three snowballs hit the windows, slithering down the glass like snot. A peal of high-pitched laughter followed the barrage. Kristen and Alicia threw on thick robes, and the four girls raced to the windows.

Claire, dressed in a My Little Pony cap and a bright red puffy coat, was pelting snowballs at Layne and their new friends—a willowy blonde and a petite brunette.

"They're ruining my snow!" Massie stared at the once pristine yard, which was now covered with LBR boot prints.

"Cheap footwear leaves the most horrible tracks," Dylan sighed. "Like the abdominal snowman."

"You mean *abominable* snowman," Kristen corrected.

Dylan pinched some snow off her fluffy hood and dropped it onto Kristen's head. "Takes one to know one."

"Ew, lice!" Alicia giggled, pointing at Kristen's scalp. "Let's go before we catch it," she joked, backing away.

Kristen shook her blond hair in Alicia's face.

"Ahhhhhh!"

Massie drew an *X* on the foggy window, her finger squeaking on the pane. "It's too bad we can't give Claire lice. Maybe her ah-nnoying friends would leave."

THUNK.

THUNK.

THUNK!

The girls jumped back as another round of snowballs smacked into the barn.

Todd dashed in front of the window and bowed, proud to claim responsibility for the latest round.

Massie whipped her iPhone out of her robe pocket. "Unless . . ."

"Is there a lice app?" Kristen asked, twisting her damp hair into a sloppy bun.

"I wish," Massie smirked, her breath clouding the window as she coaxed her brain into constructing the ultimate plan—a plan that would accomplish her sinister goal without implicating her sinister mind. Seven breath clouds later, she had it. And sent an urgent text to Claire's younger brother.

Massie: Come 2 the barn ay-sap. Impt.

Bwoop.

The message had been sent. Seconds later, Todd and his best friend, Tiny Nathan, appeared in the doorway. Todd looked like a freckled Buzz Lightyear in his puffy white-and-green snowsuit. Nathan resembled a poo in his three-sizes-too-big brown snow pants and matching hooded coat.

Todd sniffled. "You wanna join our team?" He pulled off his hood. His orange hair was spiked with sweat. "We're called Big Balls."

Nathan giggled. And then Todd giggled. And then Nathan giggled some more.

"No, this is nawt about joining your—"

Massie's iPhone buzzed.

Kristen: ??? R U doing?
Alicia: ??? Does this have 2 do w lice?
Dylan: Ha! Big balls. ☺
Massie: Quit bugging me. ☺ Trust me.

Massie reached for the pack of Mango Surf–flavored Orbit sticking out of Dylan's purse and popped a piece in her mouth. She bit down, recalling the satisfying flavor that squishing the competition usually left in her mouth. "I just learned a new massage technique that I'm dying to try on someone. It's supposed to increase scalp circulation and prevent hair from sweating." Massie waved away the imaginary smell coming from Todd's head.

Alicia and Kristen exchanged confused looks. Dylan snatched the pack of gum out of Massie's hand and stuffed four pieces in her mouth.

"Why didn't you try it out on Kristen, then?" Tiny Nathan pointed out.

"This isn't sweat." Kristen smoothed the wet hair on top of her head. "It's melted snow, okay?" She flashed Dylan a *thanks a lot* look.

Dylan blew her a glossy *you're welcome* kiss.

Todd's eyes darted between the two girls in confusion.

"So whaddaya say?" Massie asked Todd, putting the attention back where it belonged. "Wanna give it a try?"

"Oh. Okay." Todd hopped up onto the couch and lay down. Tiny Nathan promptly pulled out his cell phone and started angling for a photo.

Kristen shrugged her athletic shoulders. Alicia finger-combed her dark locks to glossy perfection. And Dylan peeled a flattened gum-bubble off the tip of her nose.

Massie's friends were the best that Octavian Country Day had to offer. Still, without Claire she felt emptier than Beyoncé after the forty-day master cleanse. But when betas defected to other crews, alphas didn't beg them to come back. They drove the betas further away. And if a little brother got hurt in the process, so be it.

"Here I go." Massie held her breath, stuck her hand into Todd's matted locks, and gingerly began rubbing his head. Who knew when he'd last washed it? She made a mental note to Purell before eating.

"I can feel it working," Todd muttered into the ecru linen cushion. After a few minutes, his breath became regular and heavy.

Dylan ran her hands through her hair the same way Massie was running hers through Todd's. Alicia elbowed her.

"What?" Dylan asked, her red brows rising. "Todd said it was working."

Kristen inched closer to Massie and mouthed, *What are you doing?*

Watch, Massie mouthed back. Then she fake-coughed and "accidentally" spit her gum onto Todd's head. It disappeared inside a mass of red curls.

"Oh no!" she cried, quickly working the wad into his hair. "My gum!"

Todd's head popped up. "Whhhaa?"

Tiny Nathan looked up from his phone and burst out laughing.

Massie widened her eyes in what she hoped looked like horror—and innocence. "Ehmagawd. I'm sooo sorry."

Todd stuck his hand up and felt his sticky, artificially flavored Mango Surf–encrusted locks. "I've been gummed!"

Kristen and Dylan snorted back giggles. Alicia tightened the belt of her robe.

"It's almost the same color as your hair. Maybe you should just leave it," Tiny Nathan suggested. "You could stick stuff to it, like paper clips and things."

Todd felt around the back of his head for the gum clump. "True."

Massie shook her head vigorously. "No, no, no. We can't leave it there. It's dangerous. It can"—her eyes landed on Tiny Nathan—"stunt a person's growth."

In a flash, Todd sat up. His gummy hair stood up from his head like the Statue of Liberty's crown.

"Stunting is not cool," Tiny Nathan assured his friend.

"Ooookay," Massie sighed. "There's really only one thing to do." She padded to the spa bathroom and opened the medicine cabinet. Inside was the silver-plated electric razor her dad kept in the cedar-planked room. She clutched it in her Essie Mint Candy Apple–manicured hands and returned to the main room, where Kristen, Alicia, and Dylan had settled on the couch, watching Todd like he was a monkey at the zoo.

"Now, not everyone can pull off the bald look. But you have such great bone structure. . . ." She held up the shaver and slid the button up to HIGH. The buzzing sound filled the room.

Todd stared at it, wide-eyed. "You want to *shave my head*?"

"No," Massie nodded seriously. "I *have* to."

The PC gasped. Todd's mouth hung slightly slack. Tiny Nathan took out his cell phone and pressed RECORD.

"Think about it. Bald men are so . . ." She looked at her friends for help.

"Hawt!" Alicia added quickly. "Like, look at Bruce Willis."

"Isn't he dead?" Dylan asked.

Alicia shrugged.

"Britney Spears did it," Kristen pointed out.

"So did Mr. Potato Head!" Dylan added helpfully.

Massie clicked to the Mirror app on her iPhone and held it up for Todd. "Think about how tough you'll look."

Todd looked at Massie and blinked. For a second she

thought he was going to freak out and run screaming to Mrs. Lyons. But then a huge grin spread over his face.

"And I'll be so much more aerodynamic!"

Tiny Nathan ran over and gave Todd a high five. "We can beat our luge time!"

Massie's high-glossed lips curved into a Cheshire cat grin. She held the buzzing shaver out in front of her. "Ready?"

Bean darted under the couch.

Todd nodded and sat down on a bamboo stool.

Kristen's jaw dropped.

Dylan let out a shocked belch.

Alicia twirled her diamond studs at top speed.

With one last glance at her friends, Massie lowered the blade. A tendril of bright red hair fluttered to the floor like an autumn leaf. And then another, and another. The buzzing blades mowed easily through the orange glob of gum. She carved a path right down the middle of his scalp. Then she made another path right next it, first on the left, and then another on the right. More and more hair dropped down onto Todd's skinny shoulders and then onto the camel-colored leather massage table.

"Looks like a motocross track," Tiny Nathan marveled, lifting his camera.

Alicia covered her eyes.

Massie pictured each tuft of hair as one of Claire's new friends. And with each strand she lopped off, she felt more and more like the Queen of Hearts, cutting off traitors' heads in the name of control.

"Done," she announced triumphantly a few minutes later, when Todd's head was shinier than a new pair of patent-leather Choos.

Todd hopped off the stool and hurried toward the mirror opposite the fireplace. He sucked in his cheeks, unzipped his snowsuit, and popped the insulated collar. "You're right," he nodded at his reflection. "I *do* have a beautifully shaped skull." He winked at his reflection, then rubbed the top of his head.

The Pretty Committee giggled into their eucalyptus-scented palms. They weren't privy to the intricate details of Massie's plan but were entertained by its execution nonetheless.

"Let's hit that luge course again!" shouted Tiny Nathan. He punched his tiny fist in the air.

"Wait!" Massie stopped Todd by the door. "It's too cold to go out without hair." She reached into one of Dylan's shopping bags and took out the baby blue cashmere Claire hat.

"Hey," Dylan protested.

Massie silenced her with a glare. Then she tore off the tag with her teeth, put the hat on Todd's head, and pulled the flaps over his ears. "Perfect. I actually got it for Kuh-laire. So make sure you give it to her when you're done."

Todd nodded that he would, the tassels bouncing around his chin. Massie picked up Dylan's tray of hot chocolates and handed them to him. "Take these, too, for her friends."

"Hey!" Dylan hissed. "Why are you doing that?"

"I'll get you another hat," Massie whisper-promised.

"I'm talking about the hot chocolates," Dylan frowned.

"Let it go," Massie narrowed her amber-colored eyes, arched one expertly plucked eyebrow, and peered out the window. Outside, Claire and her friends were innocently tending to an ill-proportioned snowman. A snowman that, thanks to Massie's ingenuity, would be on the Block Estate longer than they ever would. Because now, it was only a matter of time. . . .

She opened the barn door and sent Todd and Tiny Nathan back into the cold. The Pretty Committee shrank from the sudden chill that swept in, but Massie faced the freezing temperature, heated by the promise of victory. A promise that warmed her more than a back loaded with hot rocks ever could.

CURRENT STATE OF THE UNION

IN	OUT
Snow day	School day
Razor blades	Razor scooters
Baldheads	Redheads (Except Dylan. Her hair is Pantene-o-licious. Always was, always will be.)

The ground glistened like Frosted Mini-Wheats. Claire Lyons's fingers were purple. Her Florida-born toes had gone numb before she'd packed her first snowball. And she was fairly certain she had bang-cicles. But the sight of Cara Whitman making a snow angel, Syd Martinez shaking snow off herself like a wet dog, and Layne Abeley eating the bag of carrot noses—it warmed her like July.

Claire stuck one blue-button eye then one green-button eye into the head of her snowman and stood back to admire her work. Her creation wore a green plaid scarf, a long orange nose, and twigs for the arms, and it had a snow-and-mud soccer ball at its feet. "Look, it's a snow-*Cam*!"

Layne burst out laughing. Little carrot flakes shot out of her mouth. Claire grinned, happy that her friend appreciated the homage to her longtime crush, Cam Fisher, and his different-colored eyes.

"Very avant-garde," Cara said, tucking a loose strand of blond hair under her white mohair cloche hat. Snow covered her belted black military coat, and her L.L. Bean duck boots were soaked clean through.

"Really?" Syd crinkled her pug nose in concentration and turned up the collar on her vintage plaid coat. "I think if we got a pocket watch and a hair dryer, he'd be pure Dalí."

"I think . . . your snow-Cam is about to get Van Gogh'd!" Cara pulled out Cam's blue eye and pressed it into the side of his cheek.

"Ahhhh!" Claire cried in mock horror. "Get her!"

Instantly the air was filled with flying snowballs as Claire and Syd pelted Cara. After a moment, Cara spun around and lobbed a snow grenade at Claire. She giggle-jumped for cover behind an evergreen shrub, then peeked out to see Layne and Cara shaking a branch over Syd's head.

Syd and Cara, Layne's ninth-grade community theater friends, were the smartest girls Claire knew. She'd been hanging out with them for the past three weeks and had loved every second of it. With them, it was about *culture,* not *couture,* and they cared more about fun than fashion. The four of them had gone Thanksgiving caroling and had made gingerbread cookies shaped like little Claires, Laynes, Syds, and Caras. After being under Massie's tight rein for the past year, Claire found hanging out with Syd and Cara as comfortable as her favorite Old Navy striped sweats.

She crept out from behind the bush, fixed Cam's eye, and stuck it back in place.

"Et ezz peek-ture purrrr-fect," Syd said, stealing Claire's silver ELPH out of her coat pocket. She circled the snowman, snapping pictures. "I see zis as zee centerfold for *Snowteen Magazine*!" she said. "Bee-yoo-tiful, darling! Now, give me more, more, MORE. Now, less!"

Claire laughed until her sides hurt. Syd sounded like Luc Coulotte, the artist Massie always hired to paint Bean's birthday portraits.

Another snowball whizzed past her head and hit the barn's front door. As Claire watched it fly by, her eyes landed on the four sets of designer boot prints leading to the GLU headquarters, along with a tiny pair of dog-sized tracks. Just a few weeks ago, Claire's own square boot prints would have been right there next to them. But now, even though she stood only a few feet away from her former friends, she might as well have been back in her hometown of Kissimmee, Florida.

A few weeks before, Massie had launched a mission to get Claire and the rest of the PC to upgrade from their eighth-grade crushes to crushes in ninth. And when Claire had refused, their friendship had crash-landed—hard. But it wasn't until she had caught Claire karaoke-ing with her new friends that Massie had declared war.

Since then, things between the two of them had been icier than the Blocks' swimming pool in winter. And although Claire had IM'd with Kristen, Alicia, and Dylan over Thanksgiving break, she hadn't seen the girls, been invited to a sleepover, or been awarded any gossip points. But every time she felt a pang of Massie-itis, Claire reminded herself that Massie's friendship was like an Hermès Kelly bag: rare and beautiful, but it came at way too high a price.

Claire didn't know why Massie needed to control her friends, but she did know she was sick of being bossed around. In seventh grade she probably would have gone crawling back to Massie and begged her forgiveness. But that was more than a year ago. She was already three months into eighth grade, and she planned to spend the rest of the year having no drama with her new drama friends.

"I'm going to make a snow Robert Pattinson!" Cara exclaimed, gathering piles of snow with her arms. "Just think how beee-yoooo-ti-fully he'll sparkle in the sun."

"Won't that make Doug jealous?" Syd asked. Cara's boyfriend, Doug, was the bassist in a band called Smells Like Uncle Hugh. They lip-kissed *all* the time—even in public.

"Jealousy is healthy in a relationship. When jealousy dies, passion dies," Cara said, kneeling to pack the bottom globe of the snowvamp. "I read it on the bathroom wall at school."

Claire felt a ping of jealousy herself. All the OCD bathroom walls said were things like KATIE WAS HERE or YOU'RE UGLY!

"Me-ladies!" Todd emerged from the barn, his eyes lit up like the white Christmas lights strung around the Blocks' windows. He wore a baby blue cashmere hat with earflaps and tassels. Claire frowned. The hat was totally cute but totally girly.

Tiny Nathan bobbed behind him, balancing a tray of hot chocolates. He held them out with a shaky flourish. "They're from Massie."

Claire wasn't sure what the gesture meant. Was it a truce in the name of the Christmas spirit? Or were they venti-sized cups of steaming cat pee?

Cara, Syd, and Claire inched cautiously toward the offering.

"Hmmm." Layne lifted a cup to the sun and examined the bottom. She shoved it toward Todd. "You try it first."

Tiny Nathan snort-laughed as Todd took a big gulp. "He'll do anything a girl asks him to!"

"All clear," Todd announced, licking whipped cream off his lips.

The other girls shrugged and grabbed their cups.

"Wanna know what else he'll do?" Tiny Nathan pressed.

"Not really." Claire rolled her eyes, suddenly mortified that her older friends were being forced to hang with her younger brother.

"Okayyyy," Tiny Nathan beamed. "You asked for it!"

"No, they didn't." Todd stepped back. But it was too late. Nathan jumped up like an anxious puppy and managed to grab hold of a blue tassel. He yanked twice. The hat slid off Todd's slick head and landed on the snow with a muted thud.

"You're bald!" Claire shouted.

Layne laughed so hard, hot chocolate sprayed from her nose. "You look like a Tootsie Pop."

"Thanks," Todd beamed, and then curled his fist under his chin and struck a thinking-man pose. "Massie did it. She says my skull is my best feature."

"She got that right," Syd joked.

"Even my snow-Cam has more hair than you!" Claire pointed to the little evergreen pine needles poking out the top of its head.

Layne clasped her hands together like a caroler and began to sing. "Frosssssty the bald man . . ."

"Had a jolly, shiny skull!" Cara added.

Syd threw her arm around Cara. "With an earflapped hat and a button nose and two eyes made out of . . ."

Claire stared at her transformed little brother, rage fizzing through her veins like shaken Coke Zero. But was it really anger . . . or jealousy? She used to love getting a Massie makeover.

Todd slapped his bald head. "Oh! I almost forgot." He picked the hat off the snow-covered ground. "Massie said this was for you."

Claire stared at it, her heart pounding as she went through another loop on the roller coaster that was life with Massie Block. First the hot chocolate, now this. The muscles in her hands were dying to reach out and grab the hat. To rush the barn and throw her arms around Massie and ask if the hat—a soft, stretchy cashmere—meant that they were finally going to make up. That Massie was finally going to be more flexible and let Claire make her own decisions. But her memory ordered her impulses to sit this one out. Could the girl who forbade her to eat processed sugar, hang out with Cam on a Friday night, or sit with Layne at lunch suddenly be open to change? Yeah, maybe. When Gwen Stefani tans.

Claire glanced at the barn. A familiar pair of amber eyes stared back at her from the window. Massie smiled sweetly and motioned for Claire to take the hat. Was it possible? Was Gwen was on a yacht in St. Barts slathering on the Hawaiian Tropic oil?

Stranger things have happened, she thought. *Like . . . well . . .*

Actually, Claire couldn't think of anything at the moment. She was distracted by her tingling feet, which were finally thawing with the hope of reconciliation. It had been weeks since the girls had even acknowledged each other. And a part of Claire had been numb ever since.

She studied the hat. It was soft and pale blue, the same color as her own cornflower blue eyes. She had to hand it to the alpha: When it came to knowing what looked good on people, the girl had more vision than Bausch & Lomb.

She put it on. It fit perfectly and warmed the tips of her ears. As she tied the tassels under her chin, the Massie-shaped ice block around her heart began to melt.

"It looks adorbs," Cara said.

"Totally you," Syd pronounced.

Claire grinned. She looked at the window and raised her hand to wave her thanks, but Massie was gone.

Read the rest of MY LITTLE PHONY, available wherever books are sold!

Are *you* the ultimate undiscovered ALPHA?

Visit www.pickapoppy.com and upload your video application to Alpha Academy. Tell us how talented, witty, charming, or just overall fah-bulous you are! The lucky winner will appear as a character in *Top of the Feud Chain*, the final novel in the ALPHAS series, coming in May 2011.

Welcome to Poppy.

A poppy is a beautiful blooming red flower (like the one on the spine of this book). It is also the name of the home of your favorite books.

Poppy takes the real world and makes it a little funnier, a little more fabulous.

Poppy novels are wild, witty, and inspiring. They were written just for you.

So sit back, get comfy, and pick a Poppy.

poppy

www.pickapoppy.com

gossip girl   THE CLIQUE   *the* daughter

ALPHAS   the it girl   POSEUR

THE A-LIST
HOLLYWOOD ROYALTY

SECRETS OF MY
HOLLYWOOD LIFE